Tricksters in the Twilight

Tricksters in the Twilight

Fox and Tanuki Tales from Japan

Kyokai,
Kenji Miyazawa,
Nankichi Niimi,
Kotaro Tanaka,
and Kohei Tsuchida

English Translations by
Finlay Cameron and John McLean

MATATABI PRESS

MATATABI PRESS (910554), a subdivision of MATATABI HOLDINGS
Windwhistle, Farley Hill, Matlock, DE4 3LL, UK
20-20, 5-Chome, Yamamoto-shinmachi, Asaminami-ku, Hiroshima, 731-0139, Japan
Website: https://www.press.matatabi-japan.com/
Email: press@matatabi-japan.com | Tel: 0081-(0)70-8592-2501

https://www.press.matatabi-japan.com/
https://www.holdings.matatabi-japan.com/
Email: press@matatabi-japan.com
Tel: 0081-(0)70-8592-2501

Tricksters in the Twilight delves into the captivating world of Japanese folklore, where tales of shape-shifting beings blur the lines between reality and legend. This collection showcases stories of two prominent *tricksters*: the cunning fox (*kitsune*) and the playful *tanuki* (raccoon dog), both embodying themes of transformation, trickery, and spiritual transcendence.

The fox, revered for its intelligence and mystical abilities, shares a sacred connection with the Shinto deity Inari, acting as guardians of fertility and rice crops. From benevolent guides to mischievous *tricksters*, foxes explore the duality of good and evil through their shape-shifting prowess. The *tanuki*, on the other hand, *often* enchants with its jovial demeanor, symbolizing prosperity and good fortune. With their playful shape-shifting antics and whimsical pranks, *tanuki* impart lessons of humility and generosity, often through clever deceit in their interactions with humans.

Many of the stories within this collection find their roots in Japan's ancient indigenous belief system, Shinto, celebrated for its deep reverence for nature spirits and animistic practices. These traditions have heavily influenced notable works such as the 9th-century compilation *Nihon Ryouiki* by the Buddhist monk Kyokai. By skillfully melding Shinto beliefs with Buddhist teachings, Kyokai created a lasting legacy, as exemplified by his tale *Fox Consort: A Union Transcending Worlds*, showcased in Chapter 1. This narrative explores themes of metamorphosis, desire, and the boundary of reality and myth. It offers a glimpse into Japanese folklore and invites readers to venture into a world where the mundane intersects with the extraordinary.

Chapters 2 to 5 of *Tricksters in the Twilight* feature fox and *tanuki* tales from four distinguished Japanese authors at the cusp of the 20th century: Kenji Miyazawa, Nankichi Niimi, Kotaro Tanaka, and Kohei Tsuchida. Miyazawa introduces readers to his signature mix of fantastical storytelling, deep philosophy, and appreciation for nature. Niimi's tales delve into universal themes of heartfelt connections amidst sorrow and the intrinsic beauty of life, drawing from his personal experiences and surroundings. Tanaka, celebrated for his romantic narratives, ghostly tales, and travelogues, brings stories from both Japanese and Chinese traditions into the collection, while Tsuchida captivates with his artful portrayal of a young fox, offering a rich and intriguing glimpse into its mystical world.

In preparing this collection, both translators, Finlay Cameron and John McLean, have strived to remain faithful to the original authors, preserving the essence and subtleties of culturally specific words, phrases, and concepts. Sub-notes are used when necessary to clarify words or phrases that might not directly translate into English without losing their cultural significance. In the translation process, the Hepburn Romanization system was utilized to accurately represent Japanese words and maintain the authenticity of the original text.

Enjoy the journey!

CONTENTS

CONTENTS

Part 1: Kyokai

Buddhist monk Kyokai emerged as a prominent figure in Japanese Buddhism during the culturally rich Heian Era (794-1185). He was a devoted disciple under the tutelage of the esteemed Jikaku Daishi (*Ennin*), a leading authority in the Tendai school of Buddhism, renowned for his scholarly pursuits and extensive journeys to China to study.

Kyokai played a pivotal role in the propagation of Buddhism in Japan. Notably, he is celebrated for his significant contributions in compiling the *Nihon Ryouiki*, Japan's oldest collection of Buddhist narratives, authored between 787 and 824. Known in English as the *Record of Miraculous Events in Japan*, it consists of three volumes containing 116 tales, including *Fox Consort: A Union Transcending Worlds*, which is featured in this opening chapter, along with nine poems. This collection underscores Kyokai's enduring legacy of preserving and disseminating Buddhist wisdom and teachings.

Nihon Ryouiki is said to be a valuable source for understanding the cultural and religious landscape of Heian Japan. The text reflects a blend of Buddhist principles with indigenous Japanese Shinto beliefs and folklore. There are five existing manuscripts, with two designated as National Treasures: the *Kofuku-ji* manuscript (904) and the *Raigo-in* manuscript (late Heian Era). The discovery of the *Raigo-in* manuscript in 1973 was crucial for reconstructing the complete text from the existing incomplete manuscripts.

Fox Consort: A Union Transcending Worlds

Written by Kyokai

Translated by John McLean

Long ago, during the reign of *Emperor Kinmei*[1], a man from Ohno District in *Mino Province*[2] roamed aimlessly in search of a life partner. Serendipity led him to a desolate field where he encountered a strikingly beautiful woman, unlike any he had ever seen. Their initial exchange was playful, with the woman showing interest and the man reciprocating.

As their conversation deepened, the man learned that the woman was also on a quest for the perfect match. With a bold request, he proposed that she become his wife, to which she agreed. Their union led them back to the man's abode, where they exchanged marriage vows.

On a frosty December day, the woman bore a son, while co-incidentally their dog gave birth to a litter of puppies. Among the playful pups was one that exhibited constant hostility towards the woman, growling and baring its teeth. Troubled by this unusual behavior, she beseeched her husband to kill the aggressive dog, a plea he adamantly refused. The tension escalated as events took an unexpected turn in the ensuing months.

In the tranquil months of February and March, as the couple prepared to *mill their rice*[3], a peculiar incident unfolded. The woman, in a bid to offer refreshments to the rice pounders, found herself pursued by the same antagonistic dog. Panic mounted, and in a swift moment of terror, she leaped out of a window, undergoing a startling transformation back into her true form—a fox. Witnessing this mystical revelation, her husband's response was one of both acceptance and longing.

Acknowledging their shared parenthood, the husband extended an open invitation to his wife, beckoning her to *kitsu* (come) and *ne* (sleep) with him every night. They soon welcomed another child into their lives, who bore the surname "Kitsune-no-Atai" and was renowned for his remarkable swiftness akin to that of a flying bird. Kitsune's extraordinary abilities and lineage harked back to the very roots of the surname "Kitsune" (fox) in Mino Province, spinning a tale of metamorphosis, familial bonds, and enduring folklore.

One day, sensing her time among humans had come to an end, the fox-woman chose to return to the world she came from. As she bid her final farewell, departing in a distinctive red-hemmed skirt, the lingering notes of lovesick songs echoed in her wake.

(1) *Emperor Kinmei*, traditionally recognized as the 29th emperor of Japan, reigned from 539 to 571 AD, marking the early Asuka Era. His reign is particularly notable for the introduction of Buddhism to Japan from the Korean kingdom of Baekje, a pivotal event that significantly influenced Japanese culture, art, and government. During this time,

Chinese writing and mainland Asian cultural elements began to integrate into Japanese society. *Kinmei* was a member of the Yamato dynasty, the ruling family that continues to this day. The construction of the first Buddhist temples in Japan also began during or shortly after his reign. Much of what is known about *Emperor Kinmei* comes from ancient records like the *Nihon Shoki* and *Kojiki*, although these accounts blend historical facts with myths and legends.

(2) ***Mino Province*** was located in the central part of Japan's main island, Honshu. Today, this area corresponds to parts of Gifu Prefecture, Aichi Prefecture, and Mie Prefecture. It was known for its scenic beauty, historical significance, and cultural heritage.

(3) In Japan, the ***rice milling*** process typically occurs in early spring following the autumn harvest, preparing the rice for cooking and consumption throughout the year. The freshly harvested rice grains are processed to remove the outer husk or bran, resulting in polished white rice.

Part 2: Kenji Miyazawa

Kenji Miyazawa (1896-1933) stands out as luminary in Japanese literature, renowned for his profound poetry, enchanting fairy tales, and deep-rooted compassion for humanity and nature. Born in Iwate Prefecture, Japan, Miyazawa's life journey was marked by a fusion of creative genius, spiritual exploration, and unwavering dedication to social welfare and agricultural pursuits.

Throughout his literary career, Miyazawa crafted a distinctive voice that continues to resonate with readers to this day. His writing, characterized by a unique blend of fantasy, folklore, and metaphysical musings, transcends traditional boundaries to delve into the profound beauty of existence and the interconnectedness of all living beings. This ability to weave fantastical narratives with profound philosophical insights and a deep reverence for the natural world has secured Miyazawa's enduring influence on Japanese literature.

Miyazawa's fantastical story *The Fox and the Earth God*, included in this chapter, centers around a serene meadow clearing with a solitary birch tree, accompanied by an Earth God from the nearby valley and a fox from the southern regions of the meadow. An evening rendezvous under the summer stars unfolds a tale between the fox and the birch tree, sparking conversations about celestial wonders and a well-intended yet deceitful promise. As offerings from humans diminish, the Earth God grapples with unspoken emotions, leading to both mischievous distractions and a poignant internal struggle. Meanwhile, tensions and misunderstandings brew among these interconnected beings, enticing readers to unravel the intricacies of relationships and emotions within this poignant narrative.

The Fox and the Earth God

Written by Kenji Miyazawa

Translated by Finlay Cameron

One

At the northern edge of the expansive meadow, an elevated clearing stretched into the distance. Abundant in foxtail grass, a solitary, beautiful birch tree stood at its heart. Though not grand in size, its trunk gleamed in glossy black, its branches elegantly sprawled, adorned with white clouds in May and showered with golden, crimson, and various leaves in autumn. Thereupon, migratory birds like cuckoos and white-eyes, as well as small sparrows and meadow buntings, all perched on this tree. However, if young hawks or falcons circled the tree, the small birds never approached, always keeping their distance after spotting them from afar.

Within this meadow resided two of the tree's companions: an Earth God dwelling in a chaotic valley about five hundred paces away, and a chestnut-hued fox that regularly traversed from the southern tracts of the clearing.

The birch tree favored the fox more so than the Earth God, for though bearing the moniker of a deity, the Earth God's demeanor was coarse; with ragged, cotton-like hair, eyes ablaze in red, attire resembling *wakame seaweed*[4], perennially shoeless, and adorned with long, ebony nails, he cut a fearsome figure. In contrast, the fox exuded an air of grace and seldom engaged in actions that provoked or perturbed others.

Yet, upon closer scrutiny, the Earth God personified honesty, while the fox's nature harbored a trace of deceit.

(4) *Wakame seaweed* is a type of dark green, edible seaweed with a slightly sweet, delicate flavor and silky texture. Commonly used in Japanese cuisine, it's found in soups, salads, and snacks.

Two

One early summer evening, the birch tree, draped in tender new leaves that exuded a sweet fragrance, gazed up at the glistening Milky Way, a canvas of twinkling stars that danced and faded in the night sky. In this tranquil setting, the fox relaxed comfortably beneath the birch tree, leisurely flipping through a book of poems. Dressed in a smart navy blue suit and distinctive red leather shoes that clicked with each step, he remarked, "Isn't it a tranquil evening?"

"Indeed," replied the softly spoken birch tree.

"Do you see the scorpion-fly up there? In ancient China, it was likened to a fiery spark in the heavens," the fox shared.

"Wasn't that how they referred to Mars?" inquired the birch tree.

"No, Mars is a planet, while that celestial entity is a magnificent star," clarified the fox.

Curious, the birch tree asked, "What distinguishes a planet from a star?"

Explaining patiently, the fox shared, "Planets are stars that do not radiate light on their own. They only appear to gleam when illuminated by external sources. Stars, however, radiate light independently. Naturally, the sun is a prominent fixed star. Despite its grandeur and brilliance, distant observers might still perceive it as a mere twinkle among countless stars."

"Ah, so the sun is also a star! It's fascinating to see numerous suns and stars above, and the notion of multiple suns is rather intriguing," marveled the birch tree.

Chuckling warmly, the fox nodded in agreement, "Absolutely."

"Why do some stars appear red, yellow, or green?" questioned the birch tree.

With a light-hearted laugh and a grand gesture, raising his arms high, the fox explained, "The universe of stars began as a vast cloud of potential. Today, a diverse array of celestial wonders graces our sky. Notably, constellations like Andromeda, Orion, and Canis Major each host unique stellar displays. Canis Major, famously known for its spiral formation, features phenomena such as the Ring Nebula or Fish-mouth Nebula, resembling a fish's gaping maw. The night sky teems with such heavenly spectacles."

"I dream of witnessing such marvels someday. Visualizing a star shaped like a fish's mouth sounds enchanting," expressed the birch tree.

"That's truly magnificent. I once beheld such celestial wonders at the *Mizusawa Observatory*[5]," the fox shared.

Eagerly, the birch tree chimed in, "I hope to behold them too."

"Let me show you. I've actually ordered a telescope from Zeiss in Germany. It should arrive by next spring, and I'll share it with you as soon as it's here," the fox remarked spontaneously. However, an immediate realization dawned upon him, 'Ah, I've just told another fib to my sole friend. I am truly inadequate.' Nevertheless, the thought crossed his mind, 'I didn't mean any harm—I simply aimed to bring joy.' Contemplating this dilemma, the fox planned, 'I will eventually reveal the truth.'

Unaware of this internal conflict, the birch tree responded with genuine delight, "I'm truly grateful. Your kindness knows no bounds."

Responding with a tinge of melancholy, the fox continued, "Yes, and I'd go to great lengths for your sake. Would you care to peruse this collection of poems? It originates from a man named Heine; while translated, the work is exceptionally well executed."

"May I borrow it?" queried the birch tree.

"Indeed, be my guest—take your time. Now, I must convey one more thing," the fox reflected earnestly.

"About the colors of the stars," interjected the birch tree.

"Ah, yes, but let's save that discussion for another time. I mustn't linger too long," asserted the fox warmly.

"That's completely alright."

"I'll return another time, so farewell." With swift steps, the fox departed, leaving the birch tree to peacefully leaf through the abandoned collection of poems under the faint glimmer of the Milky Way. The anthology brimmed with melodies, captivating the birch tree's attention throughout the night. As the clock passed three in the meadow, the Golden Bird Palace emerged slowly in the east, marking the start of a new day.

The night faded, and the bright sun rose. Dew glistened on the grass, and flowers bloomed vibrantly. From the northeast, the Earth God approached calmly, basking in the sunrise's golden light like molten copper. Showing great restraint, he moved closer with folded arms, causing the birch tree to adjust its rustling leaves and turn toward him.

"Greetings, Ms. Birch Tree. A fine morning," the Earth God's voice resonated calmly.

Returning the greeting, the birch tree replied, "Good morning."

The Earth God pondered aloud, his voice carrying a tinge of curiosity, "Reflecting upon it, there are mysteries that elude even my comprehension."

Intrigued, the birch tree inquired, "What mysteries trouble you?"

The Earth God mused, "Consider the enigma of green grass springing forth from dark soil or the kaleidoscope of colors adorning flowers. These are among the arcana that perplex me."

Engrossed in contemplation, the birch tree suggested, "Perhaps the color emerges from the seeds themselves, like the blue or white hues of grass seeds."

Acknowledging the explanation, the Earth God expressed continued bewilderment, "Even so, the appearance of mushrooms in autumn, devoid of seeds, adorned in varied hues like red and yellow, remains a puzzle."

"Why don't you ask the fox?" the birch tree inadvertently said, still enraptured by thoughts of previous night's starry night.

The Earth God's visage darkened at the mere mention of the fox, his fists clenching. "What knowledge could a mere fox possess to concern a deity?"

Responding uneasily, the birch tree stated, "I merely speculated, considering the fox might offer a different perspective."

Enraged by the suggestion, the Earth God's fury intensified. He paced with clenched fists, casting a menacing shadow on the trembling landscape. "Foxes are the scourge of the world. Do not believe a word that fox says; he is cowardly, extremely jealous."

Pausing briefly to compose herself, the birch tree spoke tentatively, "Your *festival*[6] is approaching, isn't it?"

The Earth God's expression softened slightly. "Yes, today is May 3rd, with six days remaining."

After reflecting for a moment, the Earth God erupted in frustration, "Humans have grown impudent. They offer no tribute at my festival. I've got half a mind to drag the next intruder in my domain into the mud's depths."

Despite trying to pacify the situation, the birch tree's efforts proved futile as the conversation escalated. Uncertain of its next move, it merely swayed its leaves in the wind. Meanwhile, the Earth God, radiant in sunlight and seemingly ablaze, crossed his arms and gnashed his teeth in restless turmoil. His mounting frustration led to a fierce growl before he departed swiftly for his valley abode.

(5) Founded in 1886, the *Mizusawa Observatory* is situated in the town of Mizusawa, nestled in the Oshu District of Iwate Prefecture in the scenic Tohoku region of northern Japan. Today, it continues to serve as a key center for astronomical research within the National Astronomical Observatory of Japan (NAOJ).

(6) The *Earth God (Tsuchigami) Festival* is an agricultural tradition held in rural areas of Japan celebrating the Earth God, who is believed to protect the land and ensure a bountiful harvest. The festival takes place in May, aligning with the beginning of the planting season. The festival typically includes offerings of rice, fruits, and other produce, along with traditional performances such as dances and music. While customs and rituals can vary from village to village, the underlying themes of gratitude, reverence for nature, and communal harmony are consistent, making these festivals important cultural markers that preserve traditional practices and local identity.

Three

The Earth God resided in a cold marsh, about the size of a small racetrack, abundant with mossy growths, and short reeds, interspersed with thistles and gnarled willow trees. The dampness of the water gave it a sludgy and unappealing appearance, tainted here and there by red iron stains.

In the heart of this marsh, resting on what seemed like a miniature island, stood a shrine crafted from logs—a sanctum dedicated to the Earth God, rising to about one *ken* (1.818cm; 5ft 11.6in.) in height. After his return to the island, the Earth God reclined by the shrine, absentmindedly scratching his black, coarse legs. Startled by a passing bird overhead, he swiftly waved it away with a sharp, "Shoo!" The bird, taken aback, nearly tumbled in its hurried escape.

Chuckling softly, the Earth God rose to his feet, only to catch a glimpse of the lofty birch tree in the distance. His expression shifted abruptly, causing him to scratch nervously at his unkempt hair, a blend of frustration and ire evident in his demeanor.

At that moment, a lumberjack approached from the southern end of the valley, following a narrow path that hugged the valley's edge. Despite catching glimpses of the Earth God's shrine intermittently, the lumberjack failed to discern the deity's form. Delighted by this ignorance, the Earth God extended his hand, unwittingly triggering an unexpected turn of events for the lumberjack as he unknowingly entered the valley. Startled by the sight of the Earth God, he quickened his steps, his face drained of color and mouth agape in astonishment.

The Earth God slowly rotated his fist, setting the lumberjack into a bewildering circular motion. Frantic and gasping, the lumberjack found himself trapped in an endless loop, stumbling and repeating the same path in disarray. Despite his attempts to flee, he remained ensnared in the cyclical walk until eventually crying out in dismay before tumbling into the water. Unperturbed, the Earth God casually tossed the fallen lumberjack to the grassy bank, where the man lay groaning, oblivious to his surroundings.

With resounding laughter, the Earth God's boisterous voice echoed toward the heavens, bouncing off the sky before descending forcefully upon the birch tree. Startled by the reverberating tone, the birch tree quivered, its leaves appearing blue in the sunlight's glow.

Unraveling his thoughts amidst frustration, the Earth God acknowledged the influence of the fox and the birch tree on his emotions, contemplating his divine nature and the unexpected ties to lesser beings. As he pondered, another hawk graced the sky, catching his rapt attention.

In the distance, gunshots reverberated akin to cavalry drills, while a beam of blue light dutifully bathed the field. The previously fallen lumberjack, now upright, hesitated for a moment before darting away toward Mount Mitsumori.

Witnessing the scene, the Earth God's laughter resounded once more, propelling his voice skyward and causing the birch tree to tremble, its leaves shifting imperceptibly.

Lost in contemplation of his surroundings, the Earth God eventually regained composure before vanishing into the dust-laden landscape.

Four

It was a foggy August evening. The Earth God felt inexplicably sad and frustrated, so he wandered out of his shrine. Before he knew it, his feet were heading toward the birch tree. When the Earth God thought about the birch tree, he inexplicably felt a flutter in his chest, deepening his sense of sorrow. Recently, his state of mind had changed significantly for the better. Despite his efforts to avoid thoughts of the fox and birch tree, he couldn't resist dwelling on them. He questioned his deific status, repeatedly convincing himself that the birch tree was somehow connected to him. Nevertheless, a sense of profound sadness remained, especially when thoughts of the fox emerged, causing an intense burning sensation in his body.

Deep in contemplation, the Earth God approached the birch tree with a mix of anticipation and trepidation. A surge of conflicting emotions enveloped him as he pondered the birch tree's potential anticipation of his arrival after a prolonged absence, evoking a sense of poignant pity. With a heart brimming with emotions, his firm strides wavered, causing the grass underfoot to tremble. Amidst the quietude, a familiar voice cut through the mist—the fox. Despite the late hour, the fox's voice carried on the gentle night breeze, softly illuminated by the pale moonlight.

The fox's voice resonated softly, breaking the silence of the night. "Indeed," he acknowledged thoughtfully. "Merely conforming mechanically to the law of symmetry fails to capture true beauty. Beauty transcends mere outward perfection, necessitating a vitality that breathes life into form. Without this vitality, beauty risks slipping into a cold, lifeless state akin to death. True beauty, therefore, must encompass not only form but also vitality and soul, resonating with life's essence and vibrancy."

"Indeed it is," spoke the gentle voice of the birch tree.

"True beauty is not akin to a fixed, fossilized model. While conforming to the laws of symmetry, it is the spirit of symmetry that truly matters."

"I indeed think so," echoed the birch tree's gentle voice once more.

The Earth God, now enveloped in a sticky peach-colored fire, felt a sensation akin to being consumed by flames. His breath quickened, overwhelmed by an unbearable torment. Thoughts raced through his mind—the brief dialogue in the field between the birch tree and the fox had unsettled his very core.

The fox continued speaking. "So, discussions of this nature are found in almost every book on aesthetics."

"Do you possess a multitude of works on aesthetics?" inquired the birch tree.

"Yes, I have quite a collection, primarily in Japanese, English, German, and even a German-Japanese compilation. The latest addition—an Italian text—is yet to arrive."

"How splendid your study must be."

"Indeed, it's quite extensive, doubling as a laboratory; scattered with a microscope in one corner, The London Times in another, and a chaos of marble seats."

"Truly magnificent," acknowledged the fox's modest yet prideful breath.

The Earth God could no longer contain his restlessness, triggered by the fox's implication of superiority. He grappled with the idea of the fox surpassing him, struggling to reconcile his self-concept as a god. The internal turmoil mounted, presenting a cascade of self-doubt and despair.

The birch tree then interjected with a simple yet poignant inquiry about the arrival of a telescope. This seemingly innocent question ignited a flurry of emotions within the Earth God, prompting him to press his ears tightly with both hands and dash forth boldly to the north. Breathless and exhausted, he collapsed at the foot of Mount Mitsumori.

His body wracked with emotion, the Earth God rolled in the grass, clawing at his hair, before unleashing a wail that pierced the tranquil night, reverberating like thunderbolts across the field. With weariness weighing heavily on him, he retraced his steps to his shrine in the early hours of dawn.

Five

As autumn gradually descended, the birch trees remained a vibrant green, while the surrounding grasses shimmered with golden hues, their swaying tops catching the glint of the wind. In parallel, the pomegranate trees boasted red berries ripened to a rich intensity.

On a day golden with autumn's brilliance, the Earth God found himself unusually uplifted. The burdensome trials of summer seemed to dissipate into a gentle haze encircling his thoughts, leaving him eager for a harmonious exchange with both the birch tree and the fox. Seeing an opportunity for positivity in their interactions, he ventured forth with a light heart.

From a distance, the birch tree observed the Earth God's approach, a subtle unease creeping into its gaze. As the Earth God neared, he extended a genial greeting to the tree, acknowledging the beauty of the day and the season's transformative grace.

"Ms. Birch Tree, what a splendid morning," the Earth God greeted warmly.

"Indeed, the heavens favor us with exquisite weather," the birch tree responded, its voice tinged with a weighted anticipation.

Discussions turned toward the rhythm of nature, where each season painted a unique stroke on the canvas of the world. The Earth God shared his contemplations, strolling through the changing landscape of colors, hinting at the blessings bestowed with the arrival of autumn's golden touch.

Meanwhile, the fox made his entrance, his demeanor shifting upon encountering the Earth God and progressing hesitantly toward the birch tree.

"Good morning, Birch Tree. I see the esteemed presence of the Earth God," the fox greeted, his attire a blend of red leather shoes and a brown raincoat beneath a summer hat.

"I am indeed the Earth God. What a delightful day," affirmed the Earth God, his spirits bright amidst the changing dynamics.

Caught in a moment of envy, the fox addressed the birch tree, delivering a promised book with a hint of a telescope viewing in the offing. With swift departure, he spared no farewell to the Earth God, leaving the birch tree unsettled and trembling in his wake.

Noticing the gleam of the fox's shoes against the grass, the Earth God's expression darkened, a deep hue of rage seeping into his features. Unleashing a torrent of frustration at the fox's actions, he was propelled into a tempest of emotions, setting the stage for a tumultuous turn of events.

As racing and roaring filled the air, the fox sprinted frantically with 'Telescope, telescope, just a little farther' echoing relentlessly in his mind. The urgency of his actions heightened the tension, driving toward an inevitable climax.

At the foot of a small, rugged mound, the fox twirled toward a round hole, poised for escape. But before he could vanish, the Earth God leaped from behind, sweeping the fox into his grasp with an eerie calmness underlying his actions.

In a sudden outburst of anger, the Earth God flung the fox to the ground and ruthlessly stomped on him. Filled with relentless fury, he then leaped into the fox's burrow, where the dim, barren interior was punctuated by the bold presence of a brownish-green spiderwort, symbolic of resilience and adaptability. As he emerged, his expression fraught with distress, the Earth God found himself contemplating the presence of the spiderwort nestled within the folds of the fox's raincoat. Overwhelmed by a tumult of emotions, he unleashed a gut-wrenching cry, tears cascading down his face like a torrent onto the motionless fox, whose serene countenance belied the depth of his untimely demise.

Part 3: Nankichi Niimi

Nankichi Niimi (1913-1943), known as the Japanese Hans Christian Andersen, emerged from a childhood marred by solitude and loss. At the tender age of four, tragedy struck when his mother passed away. This led to his adoption by his maternal grandparents four years later. Yet, despite these early hardships, Niimi's creative talent blossomed during his junior high school years, ultimately culminating in the publication of his debut work, *Gon, the Mischievous Fox*, included in this chapter, when he was merely 18 years old.

Niimi's dedication to crafting tales that resonate with humor and pathos reflects the enduring influence of his upbringing in Handa City, Aichi Prefecture. Although he began studying English literature at the Tokyo University of Foreign Studies, illness caused him to withdraw from the program and return to Handa City, where he served as a teacher at a girls' high school while fervently pursuing his writing aspirations.

The tender connections he shared with his mother and the poignant landscapes of his hometown provided a vivid backdrop for Niimi's narratives. His understanding of universal themes—the meeting of hearts amidst sorrow and the inherent beauty of life— found expression in many of his works. Despite his untimely passing in 1943 at the age of 29 due to tuberculosis, Niimi's legacy endured through a posthumous release of his extensive literary works.

The *Niimi Nankichi Memorial Museum* in Handa honors the celebrated author, showcasing his manuscripts, diaries, and a diorama display. The museum's unique wavy design mirrors the Chita Peninsula's landscape, which serves as a backdrop for Niimi's tales. Nearby, pathways through nature echo settings from his works, including the Nakayama Castle ruins featured in *Gon, the Mischievous Fox.*

Fox Spirits

Written by Nankichi Niimi

Translated by Finlay Cameron

One

Seven children, some young and some old, walked together on a moonlit night, each one illuminated by the gentle glow of the moon above. Their shadows, short and squat, sprawled on the ground beneath them.

As they gazed at their shadows, the children noticed how disproportionately large their heads seemed and how short their legs appeared. This sight brought bursts of laughter to some, while others took a few steps forward or back, amused by their comical silhouettes.

On such a moonlit night, the air was ripe for dreamlike thoughts, and the children often found their minds wandering to fantastical realms. Eager to witness the night festival, they set off for Hongo, a neighboring village ten minutes away on foot.

As they climbed the steep hill leading to Hongo, the soft spring night breeze carried the faint sound of a flute, whispering its melody through the air. This enchanting music quickened their pace, their feet moving faster with excitement.

One child, Bunroku, started to lag behind.

"Bunroku! Come on, little fellow. Hurry up!" the other children called.

In the silver light of the moon, Bunroku's thin frame, pale complexion, and large eyes were clearly visible. Determined to catch up, he quickened his steps.

"Wait up, Guys; I'm wearing my mother's *geta*[7]!" he exclaimed, sniffing. Indeed, beneath his long, slender toes, he wore a pair of adult-size *geta*, which made his efforts all the more challenging.

(7) **Geta** are traditional Japanese wooden sandals raised on stilts. They typically have a flat wooden base elevated with two supports, one under the heel and another under the toe. They also feature a *hanao*, a fabric strap that secure the foot to the **geta**, which can be adjusted for comfort and comes in various materials, colors, and designs.

Two

Upon arriving in Hongo, the children quickly noticed a small *geta* shop by the roadside. Their task was clear: they needed to buy a pair for Bunroku, just as his mother had asked.

"Ma'am, excuse me," piped up Yoshinori, stepping forward and addressing the shopkeeper with a polite urgency. "This boy here is the son of Ms. Seisa from Taruya. Could you please give him a pair of *geta*? His mother has promised to bring the money later."

The children nudged Bunroku forward so the shopkeeper could get a good look at him. Standing before her, Bunroku blinked nervously, his large eyes wide in the moonlight.

The shopkeeper laughed warmly and reached up to the shelf, carefully selecting a suitable pair.

"Let's see which pair fits you best," Yoshinori said, taking charge like a caring elder brother. He kneeled down and began fitting the *geta* onto Bunroku's feet, ensuring a comfortable fit. After all, Bunroku, being an only child, was quite pampered.

Just as Bunroku was fastening his new *geta*, an old woman with a bent back shuffled into the shop. She eyed Bunroku and, with a sudden, mysterious tone, remarked, "I don't know whose child you are, but they say if you wear new *geta* at night, you're likely to be possessed by a fox."

The children froze, staring at the old woman in disbelief.

"That's nonsense," Yoshinori declared firmly.

"It's just a superstition," added another child, trying to sound brave.

Despite their words, a flicker of worry danced across their faces.

"Don't fret," the shopkeeper said, sensing their unease. "I'll take care of it." She mimicked the strike of a match and gently touched the sole of Bunroku's new *geta*. "There, it's done. Now no foxes or *tanukis* will bother you."

With that reassurance, the children's tension melted away, and they left the shop, their spirits once again lifted by the glow of the moonlit night.

Three

The children, munching on cotton candy, gazed in awe at the festival stage. A young performer, a *Chigo*[8], painted with white powder, twirled two fans with mesmerizing speed. The children whispered to each other, recognizing the dancer as Toneko from the Otafukuyu family.

"Look, that's Toneko," they giggled to each other.

Once the dance lost its novelty, they ventured into the darker corners of the festival. There, they set off jumping jacks that bounced around energetically and hurled small explosive pellets against stone walls, watching them burst with delight.

In the bright electric light illuminating the stage, swarms of insects danced around. Beneath the front eaves of the stage, a large, reddish-brown moth clung steadfastly.

As the *Sanbaso puppet*[9] started its dance on the narrow ledge at the front of the stage, the number of festival-goers in the shrine's grounds seemed to dwindle, and the sounds of fireworks and rubber balloons began to fade.

The children gathered in front of the stage, craning their necks to gaze up at the puppet. Its figure, neither completely adult nor childlike, had eerily lifelike dark eyes. They blinked from time to time, a result of the puppeteer's deft manipulation of strings from behind. The children understood the mechanics well, yet every blink brought a strange, unsettling feeling.

The puppet's mouth snapped open abruptly, its bright red tongue darting out before the mouth closed again. The puppeteer's magic was clear. Had this happened during the day, the children would have laughed gleefully. But now, bathed in the lantern's flickering light, the puppet's lifelike gestures—the blinking and tongue-flicking—were eerie, almost sinister.

The children suddenly remembered Bunroku's new *geta* and the old woman's ominous words about them attracting fox spirits when worn at night. Unease crept into their hearts.

Realizing they had lingered too long, they recalled the journey back through the fields that awaited them. It was time to head home.

(8) *Chigo* is a term used in Japanese culture to refer to a child, often a young boy, who serves as an attendant or acolyte in religious or ceremonial roles. Historically, *Chigo* were associated with Buddhist temples and were often involved in various rituals and performances, including traditional dances and other forms of cultural display.

(9) *Sanbaso puppet* is a character in traditional Japanese performing arts, often associated with Noh and Bunraku (puppet theater). This character usually performs a type of ceremonial dance that is meant to bring good fortune or celebrate an auspicious occasion.

Four

The return journey was also bathed in moonlight, but it felt oddly dull. The children walked in silence, each seemingly lost in their own thoughts, as if peering deeply into their own hearts.

As they reached the top of the hill, one child leaned over to another and whispered something. The message passed from ear to ear, from one child to the next, until all had heard it—except for Bunroku.

The whispered message was this: "The lady at the shop didn't actually cast a real spell on Bunroku's *geta* by striking a match. She was only pretending."

The children continued to walk quietly, the weight of the revelation pressing down on them. They pondered deeply as they walked.

"What does it mean to be possessed by a fox?" they wondered. "Could a fox really enter Bunroku's body? Would his appearance remain the same, but his heart turn into that of a fox? This could mean that even now, Bunroku might be possessed." He was quiet, so they couldn't tell, but perhaps his heart had already transformed into a fox's.

Walking under the same moonlit sky, along the same path through the fields, their thoughts grew more anxious. Their pace naturally quickened, spurred by an unspoken fear.

When they came upon a pond encircled by low peach trees, one of the children suddenly made a small noise, "*Kon*[10]," resembling a cough.

Given the stillness of their walk, no sound went unnoticed. The children immediately sought to discover who had made the sound. It turned out that it was Bunroku.

Bunroku had uttered, "*Kon!*"

The children began to sense a deeper meaning behind this simple cough. On second thought, it didn't seem like a cough at all. It was more like the cry of a fox.

"*Kon*," Bunroku repeated.

A chill gripped their hearts. The children were convinced that Bunroku had turned into a fox. The terrifying realization struck them: among their group, a fox had slipped in, and it was now dwelling inside Bunroku.

(10) In Japan, the onomatopoeic sound "**kon-kon**" is commonly associated with a fox's bark or cry. This same sound is also used to mimic the sound of a human cough. This overlapping association has given rise to a belief in Japanese folklore: One cough signifies a fox is near, while two coughs denote the fox being far away.

Five

Bunroku's house in Taruya stood a good distance from the other children's homes, a secluded abode nestled in the valley amidst expansive *mikan*[11] orchards. Typically, the children made a small detour from the watermill to accompany Bunroku to his gate, as he was an only child accustomed to being pampered. Bunroku's mother frequently indulged the children with *mikans* and sweets, inviting them to play with her son. On this evening as well, they had paused at Bunroku's gate to fetch him before heading to the festival.

As they arrived at the watermill, a narrow path veered off from its side, winding through the grass down to Bunroku's house. However, on this particular night, there was a noticeable reluctance to walk Bunroku home, almost as if they had overlooked him. It wasn't a matter of forgetting but rather a sense of apprehension towards him that lingered among the group.

Bunroku clung to the hope that Yoshinori, ever gentle and kind, would accompany him along the path. With longing looks over his shoulder, he set off on the moonlit path alone. The croak of a nearby frog broke the quiet, becoming his sole audible companion in the darkness.

Though it was not far to his home, he usually had the company of his friends. Tonight, their absence was keenly felt. Bunroku, appearing dazed, was fully aware of the whispers about his *geta* and the consequences of his cough.

The same friends who had been so kind to him before the festival now abandoned him, believing he was possessed by a fox because he had worn new *geta* at night. The thought filled him with sadness.

Yoshinori, who was four years older, would often lend Bunroku his *haori*[12] if he looked cold. However, tonight, even as Bunroku coughed, no one offered him warmth or comfort.

Bunroku reached the hedge that made up his house's outer fence. As he opened the small wooden gate at the back of the house and stepped inside, he saw his small shadow cast by the moonlight and a sudden worry struck him.

"Maybe I really am possessed by a fox. What will Mother and Father do if they find out?"

(11) The Japanese *mikan*, also known as the Satsuma mandarin, is a small citrus fruit with a bright orange, thin, and smooth peel. It is one of the most popular citrus fruits in Japan. *Mikan* trees are often planted on slopes and terraced hillsides facing the sea for optimal drainage, frost protection, and sunlight exposure, all vital for tree health and productivity.

(12) A Japanese *haori* is a traditional hip- or thigh-length jacket that is worn over a kimono. It typically has wide sleeves and is worn open in the front without fastenings.

Six

Bunroku and his mother retired early for the night. Despite being a third grader, he still shared a bed with his mother—it was to be expected for an only child.

"Now, let's hear about the festival from you," his mother said, straightening Bunroku's pajama collar as he lay down.

Bunroku often recounted his school days, town visits, and movie experiences to his mother. Despite his storytelling being somewhat fragmented, his mother always found joy in listening to him.

"The *Chigo*—it turned out she was Toneko Otafukuyu," Bunroku shared.

His mother smiled, intrigued. "What else do you remember from the festival?" she inquired.

Bunroku strained to recall the festival lineup and then diverted the conversation to something else. "Mother, do you really get possessed by a fox if you put on new *geta* at night?"

His mother looked amused at first but soon pondered the events of the evening. "Who said such a thing?" she asked, taken aback by Bunroku's question.

Bunroku repeated his query persistently. "Do you, Mother?"

"It's a lie. Stories of that sort are just myths from the past," she reassured him.

"So it's not true?"

"Not at all."

"Are you sure?"

"Absolutely."

After a brief silence, Bunroku's eyes sparkled as he inquired further, "What if it were true?"

"What do you mean, 'What if?'" his mother asked, bemused.

"What if I really turn into a fox?"

The surreal nature of the conversation caused his mother to burst into laughter. Bunroku, a bit embarrassed, gently pushed his mother's chest with both hands.

"In that case," his mother began, assuming an overly serious tone, "since you're such an adorable little boy, if you were to transform into a fox, our world would be devoid of joy. To prevent such emptiness, we would all choose to become foxes and forsake our human lives."

"Both you and Father would turn into foxes?"

"Yes, tomorrow night, we would visit the *geta* shop to purchase new pairs and transform together. Then, we would take you, our little fox, to Raven Root."

Bunroku's eyes sparkled with excitement. "Is Raven Root to the west?"

"It's located in the southwestern mountains," his mother clarified.

"Deep in the mountains?"

"Yes, nestled within a dense pine grove."

"Could there be hunters?"

"There might be one or two," she acknowledged.

Bunroku expressed his concerns about potential challenges they might encounter, showing apprehension about his role as the youngest fox.

His questions prompted his mother to share fanciful escape strategies in case they were pursued by hunters and their dogs.

Taken aback, Bunroku stared into his mother's eyes, frightened by the ominous scenario she described. "Mother, no! Mother, that's a dreadful idea!" he exclaimed, rejecting his mother's fanciful plan.

As tears streamed down his face, his mother gently wiped them away, retrieving a small pillow that Bunroku had tossed aside and placing it softly under his head.

The Fox's Mission

Written by Nankichi Niimi

Translated by Finlay Cameron

In the heart of the rugged mountains, a diverse community thrived, consisting of monkeys, deer, wolves, and wily foxes, all coexisting under the vast canopy of ancient trees. They shared a single paper lantern, a simple yet elegant creation enveloped in delicate paper, symbolizing their unity within the embrace of nature's untamed beauty.

When the cloak of night descended upon the land, they would ignite their lantern, casting a warm, flickering glow into the darkness. However, one fateful evening, a realization dawned upon them: their reservoir of oil had been drained, and they needed to replenish it from the oil shop in the nearby village.

A collective reluctance shadowed the decision of who would undertake this journey, as the path to the village held terrors they all wished to avoid. The village was home to hunters and their despised dogs.

"Who will go to the village and fetch the oil?" someone questioned, worry evident in their voice.

"I will go," offered a wily fox, stepping forward with confidence. "I can masquerade as a human child, so the hunters and their dogs won't suspect me."

Thus, the mantle of responsibility was laid upon the fox's shoulders. Little did he or any of the animals foresee the twists and turns that lay in wait. With deft deception, the fox assumed the guise of a human child, the burden of their empty vial drawing him toward the flickering lights of the village on a moonlit night.

The fox moved gracefully across the picturesque moonlit rice fields. The fragrances of the village wafted through the gentle breeze as he approached the oil vendor. Upon obtaining a vial of precious oil, he began his journey back to the mountains, carrying with him the scent of the oil's promise.

Yet, as the night progressed, the allure of the oil proved too much for the fox's self-control. He sniffed the vial and said to himself, "A little taste won't hurt." With that, he licked the oil. The taste was so delightful that he couldn't resist another lick, and then another.

"Just a bit more," he convinced himself each time. Before long, the oil was naught but a memory, leaving the empty vial as a meager memento of his journey.

Returning to his fellow companions, the deer, monkeys, wolves, and foxes beheld the barren vial, a tangible testament to their misplaced trust. Disappointment and regret whispered through the night air, a sobering reminder of the consequences of underestimating the wiles of a cunning fox.

"And so," sighed a monkey, "we should not have sent the fox to fetch the oil."

The mountain abode was cloaked in disappointment and reflection, the echoes of their missteps resonating through the ancient trees—a cautionary tale for all who inhabited the untamed wilderness.

Gon, the Mischievous Fox

Written by Nankichi Niimi

Translated by Finlay Cameron

One

This is a tale that an old man from my village told me when I was just a child.

Long ago, near our village, there stood a small castle in a place called Nakayama. Lord Nakayama was the master of the castle.

A little distance away from Nakayama, in the depths of a lush forest filled with ferns, lived a fox named Gon. Gon was a solitary little fox who had dug a hole in the dense undergrowth. Day and night, Gon would venture out into the nearby villages, not to cause harm, but to indulge his mischievous nature. He would sneak into fields to scatter potatoes, set fire to drying rape seed stalks, and pluck the peppers that hung in the backyards of peasant houses. His antics were many and varied.

One autumn, after it had rained continuously for two or three days, Gon found himself confined to his hole. When the rain finally ceased, he emerged, relieved. The sky was clear, and the air was filled with the sharp calls of *Japanese titmice*[13].

Gon made his way to the bank of the village stream, where the tips of the Japanese pampas grass still glistened with raindrops. The usually shallow river had swollen significantly after the days of rain. The riverbanks, normally dry, were inundated, causing the pampas grass and bush clover to lie submerged and struggling in the yellow-ish, muddy waters. Gon walked along the muddy path that followed the river.

As he looked down toward the river, Gon noticed a figure. With quiet steps, he moved closer through the tall grass to observe without being noticed. "It's Hyouju," Gon thought. Hyouju was a familiar figure, dressed in a tattered black kimono with his sleeves rolled up. He stood waist-deep in the water, vigorously shaking a fishing net. A single round leaf of bush clover was stuck to the side of his face, resembling a large mole.

After some time, Hyouju lifted the backmost part of the net from the water. It resembled a bag and was filled with tangled roots, leaves, and rotting wood bits. Amidst this jumble, flashes of white caught the light—the bellies of plump eels. Hyouju tossed the eels, along with the debris, into his fishing creel. Then he tied the mouth of the net shut and put it back into the water.

Hyouju stepped out of the river with his creel, set it on the bank, and headed upstream, appearing to search for something.

No sooner had Hyouju disappeared from view than Gon darted out from his hiding place. A mischievous glint in his eye, he approached the creel. He grabbed the eels one by one and hurled them into the river downstream, away from Hyouju's net. Each eel landed with a splash, quickly disappearing into the muddy water.

Finally, Gon tried to grasp a particularly thick eel, but it slipped through his paws. Growing impatient, he plunged his head into the creel and bit down on the eel's head. The eel squealed and wrapped itself tightly around Gon's neck. At that moment, Hyouju's loud shout pierced the air, "You thieving fox!"

Startled, Gon leapt into the air. He tried to shake off the eel and make his escape, but the eel clung persistently to his neck. Gon bolted away, running as fast as his legs could carry him. Near his burrow, under the shade of a tree, Gon finally risked a glance back. Thankfully, Hyouju was not in pursuit.

Gon bit down on the eel's head, causing it to release its grip. With a sigh of relief, he removed it from his neck and carefully placed it on a blade of grass near his burrow, bringing his latest adventure to a close.

(13) *Japanese titmice* are songbirds that belong to the family Paridae and are native to Japan. They are also known as *Japanese tits* or *Japanese chickadees*. These birds are known for their distinctive plumage, acrobatic flight, and melodious songs. They are commonly found in forests, woodlands, and gardens throughout Japan, where they feed on insects, seeds, and berries.

Two

About ten days later, as Gon was passing behind the house of a farmer named Yasuke, he noticed Yasuke's wife under the shade of a fig tree, meticulously applying *black tooth dye*[14]. Continuing his stroll, Gon passed by the house of the village blacksmith, Shinbei, where Shinbei's wife was combing her hair with great care. Gon thought, "Hmm, something must be happening in the village. What could it be? If it were a festival, there would be the sound of drums and flutes, and surely streamers would be set up at the shrine."

As Gon pondered this, he found himself in front of Hyouju's house, which had a distinctive red well in the front yard. The small, almost dilapidated house was bustling with people. Women dressed in their best *kimonos*, with hand towels tucked into their sashes, were busy lighting a fire in the outdoor stove. Something was simmering in a large pot.

"Oh, it's a funeral," Gon realized with a start. "I wonder who in Hyouju's family has passed away."

That afternoon, Gon made his way to the village cemetery and hid behind the *Roku-Jizo Statues*[15]. It was a clear, beautiful day, and the castle's roof tiles glistened in the distance. In the cemetery, the red spider lilies were in full bloom, painting the ground with their crimson petals. From the direction of the village came the resonant sound of a bell, signaling the start of the funeral procession.

Soon, Gon saw the procession approaching, with mourners dressed in white kimonos. The sound of their murmuring voices grew nearer. As the funeral procession entered the cemetery, the red spider lilies were trampled underfoot.

Standing on his tiptoes, Gon strained to see over the crowd. There was Hyouju, clad in a white mourning robe, carrying the ancestral tablet. His usually vibrant face, which reminded Gon of a fresh sweet potato, was now pallid and somber.

"So, it was Hyouju's mother who died," Gon realized, his heart sinking as he withdrew.

That night, back in the solitude of his hole, Gon couldn't stop thinking. "Hyouju's mother must have been bedridden, longing for eel," he reasoned. "That must be why Hyouju went out with the fishing net. But I played that foolish prank and took the eels. Because of that, Hyouju couldn't bring the eels to his mother. She must have passed away, still yearning to eat eel. Ah, she must have died, dreaming of eating eels. Oh, if only I hadn't been so thoughtless and mischievous."

(14) In Japan, **black tooth dye**, known as *ohaguro*, was a traditional practice where teeth were artificially dyed black to signify maturity, beauty, and social status. *Ohaguro* was primarily worn by married women and sometimes men of the noble or upper class. The custom dates back centuries and was popular during the Edo Era (1603-1868). The black dye was made from ingredients like iron filings, vinegar, and tea, creating a dark color that symbolized devotion to one's spouse and family. *Ohaguro* was also believed to protect teeth from decay and strengthen them.

(15) **Roku-Jizo Statues**, also referred to as the *Six Jizo Statues*, are a set of six stone Buddhist figures found along roadsides, pathways, or in mountainous regions in Japan. Each statue represents a revered figure in Japanese Buddhism, known for protecting travelers, children, and the deceased.

Three

Hyouju stood by the red well, washing wheat and shoveling it with a kind of patient lethargy. He and his mother had always led a humble and poor existence, and now that she was gone, Hyouju was left utterly alone.

"So, Hyouju is just like me—completely alone now," Gon thought as he watched from the shadow of the storeroom.

As Gon stepped out from the storeroom, a loud and lively voice caught his attention. "Fresh sardines for sale! Fresh and shiny sardines!"

Gon quickly ran toward the source of the lively announcement, arriving just in time to see Yasuke's wife at her back door, calling out, "I'll take some sardines!" The sardine seller, his cart heaped with the glittering fish, stopped and scooped up a handful of sardines to bring into Yasuke's house. Seizing the moment, Gon darted forward, snatched five or six sardines from the basket, and scampered back toward Hyouju's house. He slipped in through the back door and tossed the sardines into the house before fleeing back towards his hole. Pausing atop a hill, Gon glanced back to see Hyouju still shoveling wheat at the well, unaware of the sudden gift.

Gon felt a small surge of satisfaction. "That should make up for the eel disaster, at least a little," he mused.

The next day, Gon gathered a big bundle of chestnuts from the mountains and carried them to Hyouju's house. Peeking through the back door, he saw Hyouju sitting down for lunch, a tea bowl in his hand, lost in thought. Oddly enough, there were scratches on Hyouju's cheek. As Gon wondered what might have happened, he heard Hyouju muttering to himself, "Who in the world threw those sardines into my house? Because of them, I was suspected of being a thief, and the sardine vendor gave me quite a beating."

Gon felt a pang of guilt and regret. "Poor Hyouju. He got those scratches because of me."

Determined to make amends, Gon quietly moved to the storeroom and left the chestnuts at the entrance before retreating.

Day after day, Gon continued his efforts. Each morning, he would gather chestnuts in the mountains and bring them to Hyouju's house. Not content with just chestnuts, one day he even brought a few *matsutake mushrooms*[16], setting them down gently at the doorstep.

(16) *Matsutake mushrooms*, also known as pine mushrooms, are highly prized and sought-after fungi in Japanese cuisine and culture. These mushrooms grow in symbiosis with the roots of pine trees and are known for their distinctive spicy-aromatic fragrance and earthy flavor. Due to their rarity and unique taste, they are often used in traditional Japanese dishes such as sukiyaki, rice dishes, soups, and hot pots.

Four

It was a beautiful evening with the full moon casting its silvery glow over the village. Gon decided to wander out for a casual stroll. Passing just beneath the towering walls of Nakayama Castle, he heard the sound of approaching footsteps on the narrow path ahead. Voices drifted through the night air, accompanied by the rhythmic chirping of bell crickets, *chi-chi-chirorin, chi-chi-chirorin.*

Gon quickly hid by the roadside, remaining perfectly still. As the voices grew nearer, he recognized the speakers: it was Hyouju and another farmer named Kasuke.

"You know, Kasuke," Hyouju began.

"Hmm?" Kasuke responded.

"Something really strange has been happening lately."

"What is it?"

"Ever since my mother passed away, someone—I've no idea who—has been leaving chestnuts and *matsutake mushrooms* for me every single day."

"Really? Who could it be?" Kasuke asked, intrigued.

"I don't know. They leave it behind without me noticing."

Gon silently followed them, his curiosity piqued.

"Are you sure about this?"

"I swear it's true. If you don't believe me, come by tomorrow and I'll show you the chestnuts."

"Well, that is unusual," Kasuke murmured.

The two men continued walking in silence, their footsteps echoing softly in the night. Suddenly, Kasuke glanced behind him. Gon froze, his heart pounding, but Kasuke didn't spot him and continued on his way. The two men entered the house of another farmer, named Kichibei. From inside, the steady drumming of a *moku-gyo*[17] resonated through the night. The *shoji screens*[18] on the windows glowed with light, casting the shadow of a large, shaven-headed monk who moved back and forth, chanting.

"There must be a memorial service," Gon thought to himself, crouching silently by the nearby well. A while later, he saw three more villagers enter Kichibei's house together. The low, melodic chanting of sutras floated gently through the evening air.

(17) **Moku-gyo** (wooden fish) is a traditional Japanese percussion instrument used in Buddhist rituals and practices. It is typically carved from a single piece of wood and shaped like a fish with its mouth open. The fish is hollow inside, and when struck with a mallet, it produces a deep, resonant sound that is believed to aid in meditation and mindfulness.

(18) **Shoji screens** are traditional Japanese interior features consisting of wooden frames covered with translucent rice paper. These screens serve as partitions, doors, and windows, allowing natural light to diffuse softly while maintaining privacy.

Five

Gon crouched silently by the well, waiting until the ceremony concluded. Hyouju and Kasuke, having finished their prayers, began to walk back together through the moonlit village. Curious and hopeful to catch more of their conversation, Gon decided to follow them, treading softly on Hyouju's shadow.

As they reached the front of the castle, Kasuke broke the silence, "You know, what you told me earlier—it must be the work of the gods."

"What?" Hyouju stopped in his tracks and turned to face Kasuke, surprise evident on his face.

"I've been thinking about it ever since you mentioned it. It can't be a person; it must be a divine act. The gods must have taken pity on you, seeing that you were left all alone. They've been sending you these gifts out of compassion."

"Really? Do you think so?" Hyouju asked, a mixture of skepticism and hope in his voice.

"Absolutely. That's why you should be thanking the gods every single day," Kasuke insisted.

"You're probably right," Hyouju nodded, still looking contemplative.

Gon, trailing behind and listening to the conversation, felt a pang of frustration and disappointment. "So, he thinks it's the gods," he thought to himself. "I've been bringing him chestnuts and *matsutake mushrooms*, but he's thanking the gods instead of me? This doesn't seem fair."

Six

The next day, Gon made his way to Hyouju's house once again, carrying a bundle of chestnuts. Hyouju was in the shed, braiding rope, so Gon saw his chance and slipped in through the back door.

Just then, Hyouju looked up and saw a fox entering his house. "That fox!" Hyouju thought, recognizing Gon immediately. "It's the same one that stole the eels the other day. He's here to cause trouble again. Well, not this time," Hyouju resolved. He stood up, grabbed the flintlock rifle and packed it with gunpowder. Silently, he crept up on Gon, who was just about to exit through the doorway. With a sharp report, Hyouju fired.

Gon collapsed to the floor with a heavy thud. Hyouju rushed over, only to find Gon lying motionless. His eyes then fell on the chestnuts scattered neatly on the dirt floor.

"Wait a minute," Hyouju gasped, suddenly realizing. "Was it you? Were you the one who's been bringing me chestnuts all this time?"

Gon, barely able to move, slowly nodded, his eyes remaining closed.

Overwhelmed with regret and sorrow, Hyouju let his firearm fall from his hands. It clattered to the ground, a thin wisp of blue smoke curling from the barrel and lingering in the cold air.

Gloves for the Little Fox

Written by Nankichi Niimi

Translated by Finlay Cameron

The cold winter descended from the north, reaching the forest where a mother fox and her cub resided.

One morning, the curious cub attempted to venture out of their cozy cave. Suddenly, he cried out, "Ah!" and stumbled back, clutching his eyes in pain. He bolted back to his mother, exclaiming, "Mother, something's stuck in my eye! Please, hurry and get it out!"

Startled, the mother fox quickly but cautiously pried his hands away to inspect the problem, only to find nothing there. Confused, she stepped outside the cave to understand what had happened. Overnight, a thick blanket of pristine snow had fallen, and now, the sun's rays were causing the snow to glimmer dazzlingly. The young fox, never having seen snow before, mistook the intense reflection for something piercing his eyes.

Relieved, he scampered off to play, his initial fright forgotten. As he frolicked on the soft, cotton-like snow, the powdery flakes flew up and transformed into a small rainbow of shimmering specks.

Suddenly, a loud, terrible rumble erupted behind him. A cloud of powdered snow, resembling breadcrumbs, cascaded over him. Startled, he rolled through the snow and darted a short distance away. Turning back, he saw nothing threatening. It was merely snow falling from a fir tree's laden branches, which continued to drop delicate, silken threads of white as they swayed.

Not long after, the little fox returned to the cave, shivering. He held out his wet, peony-colored hands to his mother, complaining, "Mother, my hands are cold. They're so cold they sting."

The mother fox breathed warmly onto his hands and gently enclosed them within her own. "Don't worry, my dear. Your hands will warm up soon. Just touching the snow can make them feel cold like this."

However, she knew that the frostbite forming on her precious cub's hands was concerning. She resolved to venture into the town that night. She would find the perfect pair of woolen gloves to keep her little one's hands warm and protected.

The dark night had covered the fields and forests like a black blanket, but the snow was so bright and white that it appeared to glow in the darkness.

The silver-colored mother fox and her cub emerged from their cave. The young fox nestled under his mother's belly, peeking out with wide, blinking eyes at the world around him as they walked cautiously onward.

Soon, a faint glimmer of light appeared in the distance. The cub, eyes wide with wonder, pointed at the distant lights and asked, "Mother, is it normal for stars to fall that low?"

"Those aren't stars," the mother fox responded, her voice tinged with apprehension. Her legs felt heavy with the memory of that fateful night.

As the town lights drew nearer, the mother fox reminisced about the last time she had visited the town with a friend. The friend had attempted to steal a duck, leading to a close encounter with a farmer who pursued them relentlessly. Luckily, they had narrowly managed to escape.

The mother fox stopped in her tracks, her body frozen with anxiety. "Mother, what are you doing? Let's go!" The cub tugged at her, but no matter how much he pleaded, she couldn't move another step. Fearful for their safety, she realized she had no choice but to send her young cub into the town alone.

"Sweetheart, give me one of your paws," she said gently. She grasped his tiny paw in hers and transformed it into the delicate hand of a human child. The cub stared at his new hand, opening and closing it, pinching it, sniffing it in bewilderment.

"Mother, what's happened to my paw? It feels so strange," he murmured, examining his now-human hand in the dim light reflecting off the snow.

"That's a human hand," his mother explained. "Listen carefully. When you get to the town, look for a house with a round sign hanging outside. That will be the shop you need. Knock on the door and say, 'Good evening.' When someone answers, show them this human hand and ask for a pair of woolen gloves that fit. Never, ever show them your real paw—understand?"

The cub nodded but asked, "Why not, Mother?"

"Because, my dear, if humans realize you're a fox, they won't sell you the gloves. Instead, they'll catch you and put you in a cage. Humans can be very frightening creatures," she warned, a shiver running through her at the thought.

"Alright, Mother," he agreed quietly, the seriousness of the mission weighing on him.

Satisfied, the mother fox placed two small silver coins in his human hand and sent him on his way, hoping that her little one would return safely.

The young fox padded cautiously across the snow-lit fields, his eyes fixed on the lights of the town. Initially, there was just one glimmering light in the distance. Soon, it doubled, then tripled, and eventually multiplied to a dozen. The little fox marveled at how, much like stars, the lights of the town could be red, yellow, and blue.

Upon entering the town, he found the streets deserted, with every door tightly shut, and only the warm glow from upper windows casting golden patches onto the snowy ground below. Despite the closed shops, small electric lamps illuminated signboards above, guiding the little fox as he searched for the store his mother had described.

He passed by signs depicting bicycles, eyeglasses, and various other goods, some freshly painted, others peeling like old bark. Being a newcomer, the fox cub had no clue what these signs represented.

At last, he spotted the shop he was looking for. A large black silk hat sign, as his mother had described, hung under a bright light. Nervously, the young fox tapped on the door as he had been instructed. "Good evening," he called out.

There was a soft clattering inside before the door creaked open just a sliver, spilling a long, narrow beam of light onto the snow. The light dazzled the little fox, and he mistakenly thrust out the wrong hand—the one his mother had strictly warned him not to show.

"Please give me gloves that fit this hand," he requested.

The hatter, seeing the fox's paw, was taken aback. He assumed the fox intended to pay with leaves, as some were known to attempt. "Please pay first," he said.

The little fox obediently handed over two white copper coins he had clenched in his paw. The hatter placed the coins on the tip of his index finger and clicked them together, hearing their genuine metallic ring. Satisfied, he fetched a pair of children's woolen gloves from a shelf and handed them to the young fox.

The fox cub expressed his gratitude and began trotting back along the path he had come.

The young fox pondered, "Mother said that humans are frightening, but they don't seem scary at all. After all, even when the hatter saw my hand, he didn't react with fear or malice." An insatiable curiosity about humans lingered within him.

As he passed by a window, voices drifted out, capturing his attention. What gentle and beautiful voices they were, so serene and tender.

> *Rest, rest,*
> *On mother's breast, so grand,*
> *Rest, rest,*
> *In her hand's gentle command...*

The little fox thought that the sweet singing had to be a human mother's voice. It reminded him of how his own mother would softly lull him to sleep with a similarly tender tone.

Then, from within the house, he heard a child's voice. "Mother, on such a cold night like this, the little foxes in the forest must be crying because they're freezing."

The mother's voice responded gently, "The little foxes are probably listening to their mother's song and trying to sleep in their den. Now, you should go to sleep quickly, too. Let's see who will fall asleep first, you or the little fox in the forest."

Hearing this, the young fox suddenly felt a pang of longing for his own mother and bounded off in the direction where she was waiting.

The mother fox had been anxiously awaiting her cub's return, trembling with worry. When he finally arrived, she embraced him warmly, her joy so profound it nearly brought tears to her eyes.

Together, the two foxes made their way back to the forest. The moon had risen, casting a silvery glow on their fur and leaving cobalt shadows in their footprints.

"Mother, humans aren't scary at all."

"Why do you think so?"

"Well, I made a mistake and showed my real hand, but the hatter didn't try to catch me. He gave me these wonderful, warm gloves instead," he explained, demonstrating by clapping his gloved hands together.

His mother, astonished, murmured, "My goodness! Could it be that humans are kind after all? Perhaps they truly are good-hearted."

Part 4: Kotaro Tanaka

Kotaro Tanaka (1880-1941) was a widely celebrated Japanese novelist and essayist. Born in Kochi City on the island of Shikoku, Japan, Tanaka's literary journey began after he immersed himself in Chinese studies and took on various roles, including substitute teacher and journalist for the newspaper *Kochi Jitsugyo Shimbun*.

In the early 1900s, a pivotal move to Tokyo brought him into contact with figures such as Keigetsu Omachi (1869–1925), a leading travel writer and essayist, poet, calligrapher, sketch artist, and songwriter, who mentored him. By 1909, Tanaka's literary reputation had soared due to his collaboration on *Reinun's Meiji Rebel Biography*[19], linking him to the literary circles associated with the magazine *Chuo Koron*[20]. Within its pages, he unveiled a collection of romantic narratives, ghostly tales, and travelogues that captivated diverse audiences. His celebrated works include stories from both Japanese and Chinese traditions, as demonstrated by the six stories in this chapter.

In his later years, Tanaka edited regional histories and promoted literary culture through his editorial role at the magazine *Hakuansha Gekkan*[21], introducing readers to a new generation of writers. After passing away in 1941, he posthumously received the 3rd *Kikuchi Kan Prize*[22]. Memorials at his birthplace and nearby Katsurahama Beach, along with preserved collections of his works at the Kochi Prefectural Library, honor his legacy and ensure his influential works continue to resonate in Japanese literary history.

(19) ***Reinun's Meiji Rebel Biography*** explores the pivotal roles of Meiji rebels during Japan's transformative Meiji Restoration in 1868. It delves into Japan's modernization and political upheaval, showcasing the rebels' advocacy for change and influence on the nation's future. This work exemplifies Kotaro Tanaka's skill in presenting historical narratives that resonate with readers, marking a significant milestone in his literary career.

(20) Established in 1887, ***Chuo Koron*** is a revered Japanese literary magazine known for its diverse content spanning literature, critical essays, and cultural commentary, providing a platform for renowned contributors to engage with contemporary issues and artistic expressions while influencing literary trends.

(21) Under the leadership of Kotaro Tanaka from August 1934, ***Hakuansha Gekkan*** served as a platform for upcoming writers like Masuji Ibushi and Shiro Ozaki, serving as a focal point for a variety of literary works and critical essays until October 1943. This publication played a pivotal role in fostering talent and showcasing diverse perspectives in Japanese literature.

(22) The ***Kikuchi Kan Prize***, named after writer Kan Kikuchi, is a prestigious Japanese literary award recognizing notable contributions to literature and culture, honoring writers for their creative achievements and impact on the literary landscape.

The Mystery of the Old Fox

Written by Kotaro Tanaka

Translated by John McLean

Long ago, there was a monk named Shigen who followed his spiritual beliefs strictly, wore simple robes, and liked being alone in the outdoors rather than in temples. On a particular journey, he traveled 10 *ri*[23] east of Hoshu Castle and decided to spend the night amidst the tombstones in a serene graveyard. The bright moon illuminated the surroundings, allowing him to see clearly in all directions.

Glancing up, Shigen spotted a fox beneath a nearby tree. In a playful display, the fox balanced a skull on its head[24] and mimicked human gestures. Moments later, it plucked a blade of grass, draped it over its body and transformed into a strikingly beautiful young woman.

Just then, the sound of a neighing horse broke the silence, and a man appeared, riding along the path. Seeing him, the fox-woman positioned herself by the roadside and began to weep. Intrigued, the rider dismounted and approached her, asking, "Why are you crying here by the road?"

"I'm from Ekishu," she replied through her tears. "My husband died last year, leaving me with nothing. I am trying to return to my family, but the journey is slow, and nightfall approaches."

The rider, a soldier from Ekishu, kindly offered, "If you don't mind, I can give you a ride on my humble horse. It would be my pleasure to help you."

The fox-woman, masking delight with gratitude, accepted his offer. Just as the soldier was about to lift her onto his horse, Shigen stepped forward and warned, "Be cautious! The woman you are trying to assist is not a woman; she is a clever fox in disguise."

Angered by Shigen's accusation, the soldier retorted, "Monk, do not cast false aspersions. How dare you!"

Unshaken, Shigen responded firmly, "If you doubt my words, I shall make her true form known." He then chanted a powerful mantra and brandished his staff emphatically. "Reveal your true form now, or face the consequences!"

Under Shigen's command, the fox-woman writhed in agony, transformed back into a fox, and succumbed, blood oozing from her body. She lay lifeless among the tombstones, surrounded by skull fragments and blades of grass, a stark representation of the thin boundary separating realities.

(23) In traditional Japanese measurement, one *ri* is approximately equal to 3.927 kilometers (2.44 miles).

(24) According to Chinese legend, the fox is frequently portrayed carrying a skull on its head. This belief originates from a text, traditionally ascribed to Gan Bao, an author from the Eastern Jin Dynasty in China (317–420 AD).

A Fable of the Fox and Tanuki

Written by Kotaro Tanaka

Translated by John McLean

A fox and a *tanuki* had taken residence above the tomb of King Hui-o. Both creatures, each over a thousand years old and of mystical origin, became intrigued upon hearing about Zhang Hua, the knowledgeable and versatile governor of the Jin Dynasty. Eager to challenge themselves and create some mischief, they transformed into young scholars and rode toward the gated city on horseback.

Their journey was interrupted by Huamaojin, the divine guardian of the city, who sought to understand their intentions. "Where are you headed?" Huamaojin inquired.

The *tanuki* stepped forward and confidently stated, "We are on our way to engage in a discussion with Zhang Hua."

Despite the cautionary advice from Huamaojin, the fox and *tanuki* remained resolute, continuing on their journey.

Upon reaching Zhang Hua's residence, they entered into a spirited debate with him, managing to unsettle even the esteemed governor. Recognizing the unusual nature of these seemingly non-human youths, Zhang Hua decided to unveil their true forms with the assistance of Lei Kongchang, a resourceful figure known for his wisdom and problem-solving skills.

After listening to Zhang Hua's concerns, Lei Kongchang suggested deploying the hounds to handle the mysterious youths.

Zhang Hua summoned the hounds, expecting a reaction. However, to his surprise, both the fox and *tanuki* displayed unwavering composure. The *tanuki* confidently declared, "Our wisdom is a divine gift from above."

Reflecting on the unfolding events, Zhang Hua mused, "A spirit of a hundred years may reveal its true essence in the presence of hounds, whereas a demon of a thousand years will only manifest when exposed to the flames of a sacred tree that has endured a millennium."

"Where might we find such a sacred tree?" Lei Kongchang inquired.

"The ancient tree by the tomb of King Hui-o has witnessed a millennium," Zhang Hua replied, sending a messenger to retrieve the tree.

As the messenger set forth on this task, a child in a blue kimono materialized in the sky, questioning the messenger's origins. On hearing about the antics of the fox and *tanuki*, the child lamented, "The old *tanuki* acted foolishly and disregarded my counsel, leading to this disaster."

Ultimately, the messenger felled the tree and discovered blood flowing from within it. Setting the tree ablaze revealed the true forms of the fox and *tanuki*, which Zhang Hua swiftly apprehended and dealt with decisively.

---

* The origin of this fable is attributed to Gan Bao, an author during the Eastern Jin Dynasty in China (317–420 AD).

The Married Woman and Her Mysterious Housemate

Written by Kotaro Tanaka

Translated by John McLean

In the village of Toyoda, nestled in *Mogami County, Yamagata Prefecture*[25], lived a peddler named Nizo Kutsuzawa. Though he had a youthful countenance, Nizo was a dedicated and experienced trader, traveling between villages each day in pursuit of commerce. His radiant wife, Nao, who had once been his next-door neighbor, epitomized beauty and grace, casting a shining light in their community.

The following events unfolded in February of 1932. Nizo stuck to his customary routine, venturing out to a nearby village. However, on that fateful day and the ensuing ones, he failed to return home or even send word of his whereabouts. Agonized, Nao tirelessly searched but found no trace of her husband.

As April approached and the snow on the mountains began to thaw, Nizo made an unexpected return. When Nao saw him, a mix of relief and disbelief washed over her. "Oh, my beloved!" she exclaimed, holding him tightly as tears streamed down her face. Nizo revealed that his peddling had taken him far away, presenting the earnings he had amassed. Having eased Nao's worries, Nizo resumed his ventures with renewed resolve, ensuring he returned home to her each evening.

Some time later, during their evening meal, the tranquil atmosphere was abruptly disturbed by an uninvited intruder who barged in, violently shattering the delicate *shoji doors*[26] while wielding a club. Startled, Nao watched in disbelief as the assailant struck Nizo. To her astonishment, the man she had initially mistaken for Nizo transformed into a bloodied *tanuki*. Upon closer scrutiny, it became evident that the assailant was, in fact, Nizo himself.

It emerged that the companion Nao had sheltered since April was, in truth, a *tanuki*. Simultaneously, Nizo, while out peddling, had experienced bouts of somnambulism, unknowingly wandering in a trance-like state. Upon his return, he stumbled upon a surreal scene of his dear wife, Nao, sharing a meal serenely with a *tanuki*.

That evening, in the aftermath of these bewildering events, Nao fell grievously ill, tragically passing away soon thereafter.

(25) **Mogami County**, a former county located in **Yamagata Prefecture** in the northern part of Japan's main island, Honshu. In 2006, it merged with surrounding counties to form Murayama District. It is known for its picturesque landscapes, including mountains, rivers, and agricultural fields.

(26) **Shoji doors** are traditional Japanese sliding doors made of translucent paper attached to a wooden frame. These doors are often used as room dividers or partitions in traditional Japanese architecture.

The Tanuki and the Haiku Poet

Written by Kotaro Tanaka

Translated by John McLean

During the An'ei Era (1772-1781), in the village of Rendaiji, re-nowned for its persimmons, and located on a back road linking the *Naiku* (Inner Shrine) and *Geku* (Outer Shrine) of the *Ise Grand Shrine*[27], lived a man named Shozo Sawada. Shozo, also known by his other name Nagayo and by the *haiku*[28] pen name Rokumei, was talented in both *waka*[29] and *haiku* poetry. He was particularly famous for his *haiku* during that time and was known among his contemporaries for his distinctive style.

Preferring solitude, Shozo led a contemplative life, with his only visitors being occasional friends from the *haiku* circle. Immersed in the art of poetic expression, he found solace and inspiration within the walls of his humble abode.

One crisp autumn evening, as Shozo indulged in his musings over a warm cup of green tea, a fleeting shadow danced across the delicate *shoji* paper of his window, piquing his curiosity and wari-ness. Venturing outside, he was met with the unexpected sight of an aged *tanuki*, unfazed by Shozo's watchful gaze. Charmed by this mysterious visitor, Shozo offered it some food, and after a hearty meal, the *tanuki* departed with contentment.

The *tanuki* soon became a nightly visitor, bringing warmth and companionship to Shozo's otherwise solitary existence. Revered by the villagers for their unique bond, Shozo and the *tanuki* shared a harmonious coexistence that was treasured and respected.

Tragedy struck when Shozo fell seriously ill, his condition intensifying with each passing day. In a poignant exchange, Shozo bid a heartfelt farewell to the *tanuki*, urging it to safeguard their shared space and remain hidden from prying eyes. With a heavy heart, the *tanuki* departed, marking the end of an era. That fateful night, Shozo peacefully passed away, surrounded by the caring embrace of the village, leaving behind a legacy of mutual respect and understanding between humans and the natural world.

In the days that followed Shozo's departure, an enigmatic woman, clad in elegant attire and holding a bouquet of flowers, was sighted near Shozo's resting place. Tears glistened in her eyes as she silently paid her respects, disappearing without a trace at the approach of a curious villager. Villagers marveled at this mysterious encounter, attributing it to the spirit of the *tanuki*, and an unwritten agreement emerged: to honor and protect the bond between Shozo, the *tanuki*, and all of nature, fostering a deeply rooted harmony within the village.

(27) The **Ise Grand Shrine**, or *Ise Jingu*, located in Ise, Mie Prefecture, is a revered Shinto shrine dedicated to the sun goddess Amaterasu-omikami. This sacred site consists of the *Naiku* (Inner Shrine) and the *Geku* (Outer Shrine), both rebuilt every 20 years to symbolize renewal and impermanence in Shinto beliefs.

(28) Japanese *haiku* is a concise form of poetry with three lines following a 5-7-5 syllable pattern, typically centering on nature or fleeting moments. *Haiku* poetry aims to capture a single feeling or moment, often incorporating a *kigo* (seasonal reference) and a *kireji* (cutting word) for added depth.

(29) Japanese *waka* poetry is a traditional form of Japanese poetry that consists of a specific number of syllables and lines. *Waka* poems are typically composed of alternating lines of 5-7-5-7-7 syllables and explore themes such as nature, emotions, and the seasons.

Mujina: The Mischievous Shape-Shifter of Kiinokuni Hill

Written by Kotaro Tanaka

Translated by John McLean

It was the twilight of the *Edo Era*[30] when Akindo, a well-known merchant, found himself near *Kiinokuni Hill*[31] in Akasaka. The *Tsukiji Wall*[32] of Kishu's residence loomed to his left, while a serene moat lie still on his right. Across the moat, the dense grove of trees at the *Hikone Domain*[33] residence cast eerie shadows, enveloping the surroundings in a haunting stillness that made the seasoned merchant pause. In this solemn setting, a figure, huddled beneath a willow tree by the moat, caught his eye.

The figure turned out to be a young woman, her face obscured by her hands, silently shedding tears. Akindo, sensing her distress, approached her cautiously, whispering, "What troubles you, my dear? Do not suffer alone in silence."

Her sobs continued unabated, her face veiled from view. With a mix of concern and impatience, Akindo gently rested his hand on her shoulder, urging, "Please, share your burden with me. What ails you, my dear?"

The woman's tear-streaked face emerged from her hands, devoid of eyes, nose, or any distinguishing features. Startled, Akindo let out a gasp and stumbled up the hill towards *Yotsuya*[34]. There, the warm glow of a street stall selling *soba*[35] beckoned, offering sanctuary in the midst of the unsettling encounter.

As Akindo approached the stall, gasping for breath, an elderly gentleman overseeing the stall, unfazed by the commotion, casually inquired, "Is something amiss?"

Enveloped in the swirling steam wafting from the hot *soba*, the old man nonchalantly waved off Akindo's concern. "No need for alarm, my friend. Folks from *Edo*[36] don't fret over trivial matters. I guess you've merely encountered a being of haunting visage."

Curious, the old man prodded, "What manner of terror did you behold?"

A shiver ran down the Akindo's spine as the old man, with an eerie smile, revealed a face mirroring the faceless woman. The encounter proved too much for Akindo, causing him to faint. Legend had it that mischievous *tanuki* roamed the *Kiinokuni Hill* area, adding an element of intrigue to an already bizarre tale.

(30) The **Edo Era (1603-1869)** was a significant period in Japanese history that lasted for over two and a half centuries. It was characterized by the establishment of the Tokugawa shogunate in *Edo* (present-day *Tokyo*). This period was marked by relative peace, stability, economic growth, and the flourishing of arts and culture.

(31) **Kiinokuni Hill** is a geographical location in the Akasaka district of Tokyo.

(32) The **Tsukiji Wall** refers to the boundary wall surrounding a residence belonging to the Kishu Domain, a powerful feudal domain during the **Edo Era**.

(33) The **Hikone Domain** refers to a feudal domain located in present-day Shiga Prefecture, Japan. It was ruled by the Ii clan during the **Edo Era** and was known for its strategic importance and cultural heritage.

(34) **Yotsuya** is a district in Tokyo with a rich history and connections to various folklore and ghost stories. It is often portrayed as a mysterious and eerie location in Japanese literature and entertainment.

(35) **Soba** (buckwheat noodles) is a popular Japanese dish consisting of thin noodles made from buckwheat flour, typically served hot or cold with various toppings.

(36) **Edo**: Present-day *Tokyo*

Secrets of a Fox's Ledger

Written by Kotaro Tanaka

Translated by John McLean

One

In the waning days of the *Edo Era*, in a cozy neighborhood near Kikigaki Temple in *Hongo*[37], Shinzaburo, a wandering merchant, made his home. His work often took him to *Jyoshu*[38] to procure textiles, which he then sold to charming *kimono* boutiques scattered across Tokyo. One crisp autumn day, Shinzaburo went away on business. His wife, Otaki, their thirteen-year-old young son, Shinichi, and Chiyoko, a short, plump, elderly household manager, were left to fend for themselves.

The evening air was refreshingly cool. After successfully shooing away any lingering mosquitoes in preparation for a restful night, Otaki tucked Shinichi snugly into his futon in the back room before settling herself down to sleep in the front *tatami room*[39], typically reserved for her husband. A softly glowing lantern, adorned with a *Doshi pattern*[40], cast gentle light near her pillow. Suddenly, she jolted awake, sensing the presence of a large figure sleeping beside her. Startled and indignant, she pounced towards the figure.

"Who are you? Wake up, this instant!" she yelled.

As her hand reached out to shake the man's shoulder, he awoke with a start, offered a fleeting smile, and swiftly escaped her grasp.

"Who are you?" she called out in bewilderment as he vanished into thin air. Otaki scanned the room, puzzled.

"That's peculiar," she thought aloud. There had been no sound of sliding doors opening; how had the man managed to disappear without a trace? A sense of unease crept over her.

"Chiyoko, Chiyoko!" she called out, grabbing the lantern and sliding open the door to the tea room, half-expecting to find the mysterious man lurking there. She called out once more. "Chiyoko, I hate to disturb you, but something truly odd has occurred."

From the adjoining kitchen, Chiyoko drowsily responded, "What's the matter, Ma'am?" She emerged from behind the sliding partition.

"Something very unusual has happened," Otaki explained.

"What exactly?"

"Well, I woke up feeling something amiss, and there was a man beside me! When I tried to push him away, he sprang up and vanished. But all the doors appear to be locked, and now he's nowhere to be found."

"He's likely just a local troublemaker, seizing the opportunity in your husband's absence. He might still be hiding nearby; we must confront him to prevent further incidents," Chiyoko suggested.

Taking charge, Chiyoko meticulously searched every nook and cranny of the room, finding no trace of the intruder. She confirmed that all the doors remained tightly shut, just as they had been earlier in the evening.

"How truly confounding!" Otaki remarked. "There was definitely a young man here. He even chuckled as he fled."

"That is peculiar," Chiyoko agreed.

Feeling unsettled, Otaki opted to have Chiyoko spend the rest of the night in her room. Fortunately, it passed without any further disturbances.

The following evening, still troubled by the events of the previous night, Otaki insisted that Chiyoko sleep in the back room with Shinichi. Not long after settling down, Chiyoko, who was naturally a light sleeper, was roused by the sense of a presence. She peeked into the *tatami room* through the slightly ajar sliding door to find the man once again beside Otaki, who was sound asleep.

"He's returned," she whispered.

Reacting swiftly, Chiyoko flung open the sliding door and darted into the room. The mysterious man jumped to his feet and dashed toward the tea room.

"Not this time, you rascal!" she declared, hot on his trail.

Awakened by the commotion, Otaki sprang from her futon.

"It's him, he's escaped again, Ma'am! Please, come quickly," Chiyoko urged.

In an instant, the intruder vanished into the shadows as if he were never there. Otaki hurried in with the lantern.

"Did you notice him beside you?" Chiyoko asked.

"I was completely unaware. How extraordinary!" Otaki replied, as a bleary-eyed Shinichi woke up wondering what the commotion was about.

"So he came back again, did he? What a dreadful situation," Shinichi mumbled as he tried to make sense of the bizarre events.

(37) **Hongo** is a district located in Bunkyo, Tokyo. It is a historic and culturally rich area known for its educational institutions, including the University of Tokyo. **Hongo** is also home to numerous temples and shrines, as well as *Koishikawa Korakuen Garden*—a Japanese garden dating back to the *Edo Era*.

(38) **Jyoshu** historically refers to the area now known as Gunma Prefecture in Japan. Gunma is located to the northwest of Tokyo and is renowned for its beautiful mountainous landscapes, hot springs (*onsens*), and historical sites.

(39) A **tatami room** is a traditional Japanese room with flooring made of **tatami mats**, which are woven straw mats known for their softness and durability. Common in Japanese homes and inns, these rooms feature sliding paper doors, low furniture, and a simple, nature-connected design.

(40) The **Doshi pattern** typically consists of interlocking squares or diamonds, creating an intricate and visually appealing design. These lanterns are commonly used in traditional Japanese settings such as temples, shrines, and gardens to provide both illumination and decorative elements.

Two

In the serene morning light, Otaki woke up as usual and joined Shinichi for breakfast. An air of peculiarity enveloped her—her gaze distant, as if fixed on an unseen horizon. Shinichi felt compelled to ask her about the unusual demeanor she had displayed the previous night but found her at a loss for words.

After their meal, Otaki retreated to the *tatami room*, shutting the sliding doors tightly behind her, veiling the room from prying eyes. This unusual conduct did not escape the notice of Chiyoko and Shinichi, who exchanged worried whispers.

"Your mother is behaving oddly, don't you think?" murmured Chiyoko.

"Yes, quite strangely. Last night, someone or something entered the house without opening any doors."

"It couldn't have been a man, could it?" Chiyoko asked.

"No, I don't think it's human. A person would have needed to open a door."

"Let's hope your father returns soon."

"Yes, hopefully, the he will come back soon, and things will return to normal."

The next evening, they decided to put a lantern in the Shinichi's room and leave several sliding doors ajar to remain vigilant. Shinichi even placed his trusted dagger beneath his futon for protection.

Otaki appeared to be deeply asleep. Shinichi and Chiyoko struggled to stay awake, whispering and keeping watch over each other. Eventually, wearied by the day's events, Chiyoko succumbed to sleep. Shinichi endeavored to remain alert for both of them but soon succumbed to slumber as well.

"...wake up,... Shinichi..." A gentle touch on his shoulder roused Shinichi from his slumber. Startled, he initially mistook his Chiyoko for someone else.

"Did it return?" he asked.

"I can't see your mother. Where could she have gone?"

Shinichi hurried to the *tatami room* to investigate. "Perhaps she's in the bathroom?" he said.

Chiyoko, following behind, added, "Perhaps." Her troubled expression conveyed concern. "She should know better than to wander off with everything that's happening. Be careful, Shinichi. Let's wait to see if she comes out."

Impatient, Shinichi took matters into his own hands. "If you're not going to check, I will." Grabbing the lantern, he slid open the sliding doors and stepped out onto the veranda, followed hesitantly by Chiyoko. They approached the bathroom.

"Mother? Mother?"

No response. Shinichi opened the door and peered inside. There, in a disheveled state, lay Otaki, half-dressed and sprawled awkwardly on her back.

"Is it your mother?" Chiyoko said, peering over his shoulder.

"Oh, Mother!"

Chiyoko moved to assist Otaki, but just as she reached out, Otaki stirred and spoke. "Who dares disturb us here?"

Startled, Chiyoko withdrew her hand.

"Mother, you should not sleep here; you will catch a cold," Shinichi said, feeling concerned for her well-being.

"Hush, you fool," Otaki retorted.

Chiyoko, feeling perplexed, pondered their next move. Suddenly, Otaki sprang to her feet and darted toward the *tatami room*. Surprised yet apprehensive for her safety, Shinichi and Chiyoko followed her.

Otaki slipped into the room and donned her nightgown. "No one is permitted in here," she snapped.

Perplexed, Chiyoko and Shinichi remained outside until they heard Otaki's breathing slow into a peaceful sleep. Shinichi, troubled by his mother's inexplicable actions, was unable to rest until the first light of dawn broke through the windows.

Three

In the morning, Chiyoko entered Otaki's room to check on her. Otaki was lightly dozing, her head resting on folded arms. Speaking in hushed tones to avoid startling her, Chiyoko gently said, "Hello, Ma'am."

Otaki opened her eyes, glimpsed Chiyoko, and scowled. "Why are you disturbing me here? Go away," she snapped.

"I just wanted to see how you're feeling. Is everything alright?" Chiyoko asked.

"You're bothering me. Leave."

Having no other recourse, Chiyoko returned to the tea room where Shinichi awaited anxiously. "How is Mother?" he inquired.

"She was resting, but seemed quite off. She snapped at me once again, telling me to leave just like last night."

"How peculiar," Shinichi muttered.

As lunchtime arrived and Otaki had yet to appear from her room, Chiyoko went to check on her once more. Otaki was sat upright, lost in thought. "Ma'am, would you like some lunch?" Chiyoko offered.

Otaki glanced briefly, then averted her gaze. "I don't want anything," she muttered.

"But you must eat something."

"I said I don't want anything!" Otaki yelled.

"Alright, I'll bring something. You can eat it whenever you feel like it."

"Stop troubling me," Otaki said, waving Chiyoko away.

Nevertheless, Chiyoko couldn't simply stand idly by. She brought a tray with a bowl of rice to Otaki's side. "I'll place your meal here; eat at your leisure."

Meanwhile, Shinichi remained in the tea room, too preoccupied with his mother's well-being to join his friends who occasionally dropped by.

As the evening approached and Otaki continued to remain secluded, Chiyoko, realizing it was dinnertime, went to check on her. Otaki was sprawled on her stomach, lightly tapping her feet on the *tatami*, the table bearing signs of mangled food. "Should I bring more food?" Chiyoko inquired.

Ignoring the question, Otaki continued tapping her feet. Chiyoko cleared the dishes, prepared fresh greens, and returned. "Dinner is served," she announced.

Remaining facedown, appearing to be asleep, Otaki curtly refused. "Not interested, go away."

After Chiyoko left, leaving the sliding door slightly open, Otaki suddenly raised her head, gazed in the direction of the tea room, pulled the tray close, and began eating voraciously. Shinichi observed this unusual behavior from behind the door.

That night at around ten o'clock, as Shinichi and Chiyoko were readying their futons in the back room, they heard a strange sound from the *tatami room*. Otaki let out a sly chuckle. Thinking an intruder had returned, Shinichi swiftly opened the sliding door and entered—only to find his mother glaring back at him from beneath the soft lantern light. There was no sign of any unwanted visitor.

"What are you doing here? Don't disturb me!" scolded Otaki.

"I thought I heard laughter and assumed someone had come again," Shinichi explained.

"Him? Don't be absurd!" she retorted.

"But I heard laughter..."

"Enough!"

Crestfallen, Shinichi returned to his futon.

"Is everything okay?" Chiyoko inquired.

"I heard Mother laughing, so I checked on her, but found nothing amiss."

"That's strange... Why would she be laughing?"

"I don't know."

The next morning, Chiyoko discovered Otaki had risen early, freshened up, and brought her makeup kit to the front *tatami room*, where she was applying powder to her face.

As breakfast was prepared, Otaki remained absent. Chiyoko decided to to take her some food. As she pulled back the sliding doors, she found Otaki lying, beautifully adorned, on her bedding.

"Ma'am, breakfast is served," she announced.

Otaki made no response.

"Shall I leave it here?"

"Just leave me be," murmured Otaki.

Recognizing further conversation would be futile, Chiyoko left the breakfast nearby and withdrew.

Four

As the days passed, Otaki remained sequestered in the front *tatami room*, adamantly refusing to emerge. Whenever Chiyoko or Shinichi ventured a glance inside, they would find her in her nightgown sprawled across the floor, occasionally crawling around the room muttering incoherently. Left with no other alternative, Chiyoko diligently prepared food for her to eat at her leisure.

One day, as they sat down for lunch in the kitchen, Shinichi reflected, "Chiyoko, what do you think is happening to Mother?"

In a whispered response, Chiyoko shared, "I can't say for certain, but there's definitely an air of malevolence."

Shinichi pressed further, "What kind of entity might it be?"

Casting cautious glances around, Chiyoko divulged, "I suspect a fox or *tanuki*, an entity that is beyond human, is attempting to attach itself to your mother."

"How intriguing. Perhaps it's a fox," Shinichi speculated.

"I pray for your father's swift return…"

"So do I. Once Father returns, that creature, be it fox or *tanuki*, will think twice about intruding here," Shinichi pondered.

That evening, both during and after dinner, Chiyoko and Shinichi exchanged hushed conversations near the lantern in the tea room. They decided that Shinichi would sleep in the tea room and Chiyoko in the back room. "Let's remain vigilant for anything out of the ordinary," Chiyoko said.

"Understood. I'll keep watch from the tea room and take care of any anomalies that appear," Shinichi affirmed.

Chiyoko encouraged him, saying, "Don't succumb to fear. If something suspicious shows its face, do what needs to be done."

"I will," Shinichi promised.

Chiyoko and Shinichi retired for the night as planned.

Keeping a dagger discreetly tucked in his nightgown, Shinichi maintained a watchful eye on his surroundings, positioned on his back with the blade within reach. As the night wore on, a palpable silence pervaded. Otaki's usual cough, a result of phlegm, did not break the quietude, with only faint rustlings hinting at rats in the kitchen. Shinichi, on the brink of slumber, remained attentive.

Suddenly, the sound of Otaki muttering to herself reached Shinichi's ears. Alarmed, he scanned his surroundings cautiously, catching a glimpse of a creature akin to a gray dog with a long tail. Reacting swiftly, Shinichi lunged at the creature, dagger in hand.

A muted whimper echoed through the room, followed by an unsettling quietude. Observing his glistening dagger on the *tatami mats*, Shinichi retrieved the weapon, poised in readiness for any potential threat.

Loud barks and cries echoed from the front *tatami room*. Shinichi stared at his bloodied dagger, realizing he had injured the malevolent creature but failed to vanquish it completely. Searching the room in vain for any sign of the entity, he deeply regretted missing the opportunity to kill it, feeling the weight of Otaki's agitation and Chiyoko's unease.

Locking eyes with Chiyoko, Shinichi shared a wry smile. "Something peculiar unfolded, Chiyoko," he began, recounting the encounter with the dog-like creature he believed to be a fox.

Chiyoko nodded contemplatively. "It must indeed be a fox. Perhaps it will refrain from returning after sustaining an injury."

"Do you truly think so?" Shinichi inquired.

After careful consideration and displaying the bloodied dagger to Chiyoko, they decided to call it a night, leaving Otaki, cloaked in her nightgown, to weep quietly.

Five

Shinichi, plagued by sleeplessness, rose from his futon at the sound of horses neighing and voices conversing in the street. The early light of dawn illuminated the dew-covered garden, casting a soft glow. Shinichi fervently searched for any remnants left by the mysterious creature but found nothing amiss.

Joining him in the inspection, Chiyoko scoured the area to no avail. Opening the shutters for a clearer view yielded no unusual sights either. "There seems to be nothing," she noted.

Picking up Shinichi's dagger for a closer inspection, she confirmed the presence of dark red residue on the blade. "It's undoubtedly blood," she remarked.

Recalling the muted whimper that had echoed out when thrust his dagger, Shinichi pondered, "It definitely cried when I thrust the blade into it. But where could it have vanished to?"

Adjacent to the backyard, the temple precinct stood, bordered by a neglected bamboo fence riddled with holes from years of disrepair. This area, adorned with various trees like oaks, maples, and camellias, served as a serene *pagoda*[41] setting.

"I'll head toward the temple," Shinichi thought.

Venturing toward the temple, Shinichi was accompanied by the gentle morning breeze that stirred the grass beside the fractured bamboo fence. Led by his intimate knowledge of the surroundings, he made his way towards the stone monuments and *pagodas* nestled within the graveyard, their serenity interrupted by the lively chirping of birds. Despite meticulously searching for any signs of blood, he only discovered glistening dewdrops on the grass and the delicate bellflowers adorning the graves.

Returning home, Shinichi found Chiyoko busy in the kitchen.

"Chiyoko, neither the temple nor the surrounding area held any clues," he informed her.

"Are you certain?" she contemplated.

With breakfast prepared, Chiyoko checked on Otaki, finding her in peaceful slumber.

"Ma'am, you seem to be resting well today. Perhaps the malevolent presence has departed," she mused, though cautiously adding, "We shall know for certain tonight."

Remaining on her futon throughout the day, Otaki maintained an unusually tranquil demeanor. Chiyoko quietly brought her meals, unnoticed by Otaki, reassuring her that the night would bring clarity.

That evening, over dinner, Chiyoko expressed her hopes for the absence of the sinister presence. "I hope it's truly gone this time," she said.

"It wouldn't dare return again," Shinichi affirmed.

As night fell, Shinichi bedded down in the tea room while Chiyoko slept in the back room. Fearing a possible visitation from the malevolent creature, Shinichi discreetly concealed his dagger and kept a vigilant watch over his mother. Eventually succumbing to sleep, he awoke to the morning light.

"Shinichi, are you awake?" Chiyoko inquired as dawn broke.

"How is mother?" Shinichi asked.

"She remained quietly on her futon all night without uttering a word," Chiyoko reported.

"Nothing out of the ordinary then?" Shinichi sought confirmation.

"Nothing. The spirit must have departed. It should only be a matter of days before your mother is back to normal," Chiyoko reassured.

Still unconvinced, Shinichi visited his nearby friend Yoshi later that afternoon. Yoshi, a fishmonger's son, was surprised to see Shinichi. "Hey, Shinichi! It's been a while. How have you been?"

Explaining his absence, Shinichi shared, "My mother was possessed by a fox, so I stayed away."

"A fox possessed her? Really?" Yoshi responded incredulously.

"I'm not jesting. I even wounded it," Shinichi revealed.

"You actually harmed a fox? That's quite a claim," Yoshi reacted.

"It escaped. I really wish I had killed it," Shinichi said.

"Have you thought about using *Ginzan Rat Poison*[42]?" Yoshi proposed.

"Good idea. I've got some at home," Shinichi replied.

After spending a few hours with Yoshi, Shinichi's concern for his mother grew, prompting him to return home.

(41) The Japanese *pagoda* is a tiered tower with multiple eaves found in Buddhist temple complexes. Derived from Indian stupas, these structures are traditionally made of wood and serve religious purposes. They typically have an odd number of stories, often five, symbolizing the five elements of Buddhist cosmology: earth, water, fire, wind, and void.

(42) In the Edo Era (1603-1868), *Ginzan Rat Poison* was made by roasting arsenic-containing pyrite mined with copper in the Saganotani copper mine in Iwami Province. Its main component was arsenic trioxide. Although not produced at *Iwami Ginzan* (Iwami Silver Mine), it was widely used and named *Ginzan Nezumi Tori* (lit.: *Ginzan Rat Catcher*) due to the fame of the silver mine.

Six

Over successive nights, Otaki continued to hide away in the front *tatami room*, exhibiting no further signs of suspicious behavior. Shinichi, on the other hand, was restless. He couldn't shake his remorse for letting the creature elude him. The eerie bloodstains on the dagger and Yoshi's suggestion about *Ginzan Rat Poison* weighed heavily on his mind.

Lost in thoughts about the mysterious creature, Shinichi felt drawn to the temple's *pagoda* area one windless evening, bathed in the gentle red glow of the sunset. Amidst the stone monuments, he stumbled upon a large flat stone askew, almost obscured by the reeds. A long, slender beast resembling a dog with brown fur lay perched upon it, engrossed in what appeared to be a ledger. Startling the beast with a sudden shout, Shinichi watched as it swiftly darted off, disappearing behind a nearby stone monument.

Intrigued by the creature's behavior, Shinichi hurried to the flat stone and discovered a ledger left behind. The pages, faintly inscribed with characters resembling *katakana*[43], listed various names such as Taka, Oyuki, and Ohana. A triangular mark stood out over certain characters on the second page, leading to the name Otaki.

"Otaki," Shinichi echoed, recognizing his mother's name. Realizing the connection between the mysterious creature and the events at his home, he concluded that the creature he had fought was indeed a fox, not a dog, as he had initially thought. Determined to confront it with this newfound knowledge, he planned to use *Ginzan Rat Poison*, as advised by Yoshi, and resolved to embark on this mission alone.

Placing the ledger under his arm, Shinichi returned home, intent on keeping his intentions to himself. Upon arriving home, he heard voices from the tea room. Expecting a visitor, he was surprised to see his father, Shinzaburo, engaged in conversation with Chiyoko.

"Hello, Father," he called out.

"Oh, Shinichi."

After hearing about Otaki's unsettling behavior and Shinichi's courageous actions, Shinzaburo patted his son's head affectionately. "Your actions were very commendable, son. I'll deal with it now. It sounds like your mother may need spiritual intervention."

Nodding in agreement, Shinichi withheld the detail about his encounter with the fox and the ledger from his father.

"Let me see how she's doing." Shinzaburo proposed, heading to the front *tatami room.*

Otaki lay motionless, unresponsive to Shinzaburo's inquiries. Her silence showed no signs of improvement. Deciding to let her rest for the time being, Shinzaburo rejoined Shinichi and Chiyoko in the tea room.

"She's much better than she was," Chiyoko said.

"Really? In what way?" Shinzaburo asked.

"Now, she responds with a glance instead of turning away."

After dinner, Shinzaburo and Shinichi retired to the back room for the night, while Chiyoko stayed in the tea room. Once again, the night passed uneventfully for Otaki.

The next morning, Shinzaburo checked on Otaki but got no response; she remained still on the futon. Deciding to let her rest and discuss the matter later, he returned to the tea room to join Shinichi and Chiyoko.

(43) *Katakana* is one of the three writing systems used in the Japanese language, alongside *hiragana* and *kanji*. It consists of 46 basic characters, which are based on simplified segments

of more complex *kanji* characters. **Katakana** is primarily used for the transcription of foreign words into Japanese, the writing of loan words, onomatopoeia, technical and scientific terms, as well as names of plants, animals, and minerals.

Seven

Beneath the brilliance of the evening moon, Shinichi ventured back to the temple's *pagoda*. Pretending to visit Yoshi's home after dinner, he wandered aimlessly around the temple grounds until the opportune hour approached. A dagger discreetly concealed and *Ginzan Rat Poison* at the ready, Shinichi contemplated his strategy to confront the fox. The night air was filled with the hum of insects, resembling the sound of falling raindrops, as shadows danced beneath the stone monuments illuminated by the moonlight. Shinichi moved cautiously among them, creating barely a whisper.

A rustling interrupted the quietude, prompting Shinichi to pause, attentive to the human-like footsteps nearing. Wisely opting for stealth, he concealed himself behind a stone monument and observed the approaching figure.

As the steps drew closer, a young man with lips painted in contrasting *red* and *white*[44] settled among the weeds nearby, intriguing Shinichi with his appearance and the absence of a visible sword. This prompted Shinichi to ponder the purpose of this late-night encounter. Soon, more footsteps approached, leading to a lively exchange between two figures. Yet despite his close observation, the content of their conversation eluded him.

Their animated conversation continued over dinner, their every word and gesture cloaked in intrigue. Despite observing intently, Shinichi could neither discern what they were saying nor what they were eating. As the evening unfolded, the chatter among the men persisted, perplexing him.

Suddenly, a fleeting sensation prompted Shinichi to shift position, and in that moment, the men vanished without a trace. Alarmed by their sudden disappearance, he inspected the spot where they had been, discovering discarded fish bones strewn about. Perplexed by this discovery, Shinichi headed home.

At home, Shinzaburo welcomed Shinichi's return. Together, they entered Chiyoko's room. Later that night, Shinzaburo was roused by Otaki's laughter. Investigating, he found Otaki on the adjoining veranda, partially dressed and emotionally charged.

As Shinzaburo entered the room, Otaki abruptly leapt toward him in attack. When he evaded her, she fell face down onto the futon, crying out loudly, "It hurts, it hurts. Why are you causing me so much pain?"

Shinichi, having woken up, stood nearby. "Father, the fox has returned, hasn't it?"

"Yes, it must be the fox," Shinzaburo confirmed.

The following day, Shinzaburo traveled to Shimotani to seek out a priest who could perform spiritual intervention through prayer, hoping for Otaki's recovery. Meanwhile, Shinichi, inspired by the events of the previous night, head out with fried bean curd laced with *Ginzan Rat Poison*.

That evening, Otaki slumbered serenely. Shinzaburo and Chiyoko celebrated what they perceived as a triumphant result of the spiritual intervention, oblivious to Shinichi's valiant actions. The following dawn unveiled a lifeless fox perched on the eaves, offering them a semblance of resolution. Shinichi welcomed the fresh day with a grin, uplifted by the recent unfolding of events.

Within ten days, Otaki made a full recovery. Shinichi's courage in defeating the fox become known and earned him not only admiration from all who heard the story but also an invitation to the esteemed Hatamoto family's estate in Surugadai.

(44) Japanese fox masks feature *red* and *white*, each with deep cultural significance. *Red* denotes power, protection, and good fortune, with masks featuring red accents embodying the protective and mischievous aspects of fox, warding off evil and bringing prosperity. *White* represents purity, virtue, and protection in Shinto belief, used in festivals to symbolize the benevolent fox spirits serving Inari, the deity of rice, fertility, and prosperity.

Part 5: Kohei Tsuchida

Kohei Tsuchida (1895-1940), born in the picturesque town of Suwa
(now Suwa City) in Nagano Prefecture, lived a life brimming with
poetic brilliance and profound hardship. Orphaned early, he lost his
father at the age of 10 and his mother by 18. Despite these adversi-
ties, his resilience and literary talent flourished.

In 1911, Tsuchida's formal education abruptly halted as familial
obligations beckoned, thrusting him into the position of a substitute
teacher at Tamagawa Elementary School. It was within the charming
landscapes of Suwa that he encountered a mentor in the renowned
poet Shimaki Akahiko and initiated his involvement in the literary
publication *Araragi*.

In 1913, after his mother's passing, Tsuchida set out for Tokyo to resume his education at Tokyo Junior High School (now Tokyo High School). Unfortunately, his health rapidly declined, prompting a prolonged recovery period on Izu Oshima Island from 1915 to 1921.

In 1924, Tsuchida's poetic voice began to reach a broader audience when he was appointed a *tanka* poetry selector for the newspaper Shinano Mainichi Shimbun. Despite battling chronic illnesses and insomnia, he continued to pour his soul into his poetry and children's stories, one of which, *The Fox's Passage*, is included in this chapter, showcasing his aesthetic storytelling style.

Tsuchida's life was tragically cut short at the age of 44 when he succumbed to heart disease. A posthumous collection of his poetry was compiled by his widow, Shigekichi Saito. Subsequent publications include a collection of his posthumous writings in three volumes (1943), a collection of fairy tales (1949), and a four-volume collection of his works (1985). His life story is undoubtedly a testament to enduring creativity in the face of adversity, making him a figure of inspiration and literary excellence.

The Fox's Passage

Written by Kohei Tsuchida

Translated by Finlay Cameron

Once upon a time, a traveler found himself wandering through the vast country of *Shinano*[45]. As he traversed a remote field path, he realized he had lost his way and eventually arrived at the banks of the River Sai. Desperate to cross to the other side, he scanned the area but found neither bridge nor ferry. He was at a loss and teetering on despair.

Just then, a voice called out, "Excuse me, traveler!" Startled, he turned to see a strikingly beautiful child paddling a small boat towards him from out of nowhere.

"My name is Konsuke, the ferryman. Do you need a ride across?" the child asked with a bright, inviting smile.

"Indeed, I do. Please, take me across quickly," the traveler replied, leaping eagerly into the boat. Konsuke deftly maneuvered the oar, and before long, they had reached the far shore.

As the traveler stepped out, he turned to thank Konsuke but froze mid-sentence. To his astonishment, he noticed a long, bushy tail dangling from the child's backside.

"Ah, a fox! A fox that couldn't quite pull off the transformation," the traveler thought, stifling a chuckle as he stepped ashore. He then casually plucked a large leaf from a bush growing nearby and, with a mischievous grin, held it out to the disguised fox.

"Well, Mr. Konsuke, here's a *koban*[46] for your service. Take it without hesitation. They say foxes around here often trick travelers by transforming, but don't worry—I won't mistake this leaf for a real *koban*. Examine it well and accept it," the traveler said, playfully.

Konsuke, looking rather taken aback, snatched the leaf from the traveler's hand and vanished in an instant. Laughing heartily to himself, the traveler continued on his journey.

As dusk settled, the traveler found an inn to spend the night. Upon entering, the innkeeper eyed him curiously and said, "Just a while ago, a beautiful child left this for you, claiming to be an acquaintance."

"I don't believe I know anyone around here," the traveler muttered, puzzled. Nevertheless, he took the box from the innkeeper, opened it, and found a letter inside.

The note read, "You must have found it amusing that I failed to fully transform. Here's your *koban* back. — Konsuke"

Inside was a flawless *koban*. Wondering whether the coin was indeed fox magic, the traveler held it over the fire, and it quickly burned away to ash.

The innkeeper was astonished, but after hearing the traveler's story, he too joined in the laughter. It is said that the innkeeper cherished the fox's letter as a treasured keepsake.

(45) **Shinano** is a historical province in the region of Nagano, which is located in the central part of Japan's main island, Honshu.

(46) **Koban** was a type of oval gold coin in Japan under the Tokugawa shogunate, which governed Japan throughout the Edo Era from 1603 to 1868. Initially worth one *ryo* of gold (16g to 18g), the *koban* was considered a symbol of wealth and power.

.

Black Tooth Dye: In Japan, *black tooth dye*, known as *ohaguro*, was a traditional practice where teeth were artificially dyed black to signify maturity, beauty, and social status. *Ohaguro* was primarily worn by married women and sometimes men of the noble or upper class. The custom dates back centuries and was popular during the Edo Era (1603-1868). The black dye was made from ingredients like iron filings, vinegar, and tea, creating a dark color that symbolized devotion to one's spouse and family. *Ohaguro* was also believed to protect teeth from decay and strengthen them.

Chigo: *Chigo* is a term used in Japanese culture to refer to a child, often a young boy, who serves as an attendant or acolyte in religious or ceremonial roles. Historically, *Chigo* were associated with Buddhist temples and were often involved in various rituals and performances, including traditional dances and other forms of cultural display.

Chuo Koron: Established in 1887, *Chuo Koron* is a revered Japanese literary magazine known for its diverse content spanning literature, critical essays, and cultural commentary, providing a platform for renowned contributors to engage with contemporary issues and artistic expressions while influencing literary trends.

Doshi Pattern: The *Doshi pattern* typically consists of interlocking squares or diamonds, creating an intricate and visually appealing design. These lanterns are commonly used in traditional Japanese settings such as temples, shrines, and gardens to provide both illumination and decorative elements.

Earth God Festival: The *Earth God (Tsuchigami) Festival* is an agricultural tradition held in rural areas of Japan celebrating the Earth God, who is believed to protect the land and ensure a bountiful harvest. The festival takes place in May, aligning with the beginning of the planting season. The festival typically includes offerings of rice, fruits, and other produce, along with traditional performances such as dances and music. While customs and rituals can vary from village to village, the underlying themes of gratitude, reverence for nature, and communal harmony are consistent, making these festivals important cultural markers that preserve traditional practices and local identity.

Edo: Present-day *Tokyo*

Edo Era: The *Edo Era (1603-1869)* was a significant period in Japanese history that lasted for over two and a half centuries. It was characterized by the establishment of the Tokugawa shogunate in *Edo* (present-day *Tokyo*). This period was marked by relative peace, stability, economic growth, and the flourishing of arts and culture.

Emperor Kinmei: *Emperor Kinmei*, traditionally recognized as the 29th emperor of Japan, reigned from 539 to 571 AD, marking the early Asuka Era. His reign is particularly notable for the introduction of Buddhism to Japan from the Korean kingdom of Baekje, a pivotal event that significantly influenced Japanese culture, art, and government. During this time, Chinese writing and mainland Asian cultural elements began to integrate into Japanese society. *Kinmei* was a member of the Yamato dynasty, the ruling family that continues to this day. The construction of the first Buddhist temples in Japan also began during or shortly after his reign. Much of what is known about *Emperor Kinmei* comes from ancient records like the *Nihon Shoki* and *Kojiki*, although these accounts blend historical facts with myths and legends.

Geta: *Geta* are traditional Japanese wooden sandals raised on stilts. They typically have a flat wooden base elevated with two supports, one under the heel and another under the toe. They also feature a *hanao*, fabric straps that secure the foot to the *geta*, which can be adjusted for comfort and come in various materials, colors, and designs.

Ginzan Rat Poison: In the *Edo Era* (1603-1868), **Ginzan Rat Poison** was made by roasting arsenic-containing pyrite mined with copper in the Saganotani copper mine in Iwami Province. Its main component was arsenic trioxide. Although not produced at *Iwami Ginzan* (Iwami Silver Mine), it was widely used and named *Ginzan Nezumi Tori* (lit.: *Ginzan Rat Catcher*) due to the fame of the silver mine.

Haiku: Japanese *haiku* is a concise form of poetry with three lines following a 5-7-5 syllable pattern, typically centering on nature or fleeting moments. *Haiku* poetry aims to capture a single feeling or moment, often incorporating a *kigo* (seasonal reference) and a *kireji* (cutting word) for added depth.

Hakuansha Gekkan: Under the leadership of Kotaro Tanaka from August 1934, *Hakuansha Gekkan* served as a platform for upcoming writers like Masuji Ibushi and Shiro Ozaki, serving as a focal point for a variety of literary works and critical essays until October 1943. This publication played a pivotal role in fostering talent and showcasing diverse perspectives in Japanese literature.

Haori: A Japanese *haori* is a traditional hip- or thigh-length jacket that is worn over a kimono. It typically has wide sleeves and is worn open in the front without fastenings.

Hikone Domain: The *Hikone Domain* refers to a feudal domain located in present-day Shiga Prefecture, Japan. It was ruled by the Ii clan during the *Edo Era* and was known for its strategic importance and cultural heritage.

Hongo: *Hongo* is a district located in Bunkyo, Tokyo. It is a historic and culturally rich area known for its educational institutions, including the University of Tokyo. *Hongo* is also home to numerous temples and shrines, as well as *Koishikawa Korakuen Garden*—a Japanese garden dating back to the *Edo Era*.

Ise Grand Shrine: The *Ise Grand Shrine*, or *Ise Jingu*, located in Ise, Mie Prefecture, is a revered Shinto shrine dedicated to the sun goddess Amaterasu-omikami. This sacred site consists of the *Naiku* (Inner Shrine) and the *Geku* (Outer Shrine), both rebuilt every 20 years to symbolize renewal and impermanence in Shinto beliefs.

Japanese Titmice: *Japanese titmice* are songbirds that belong to the family Paridae and are native to Japan. They are also known as *Japanese tits* or *Japanese chickadees*. These birds are known for their distinctive plumage, acrobatic flight, and melodious songs. They are commonly found in forests, woodlands, and gardens throughout Japan, where they feed on insects, seeds, and berries.

Jyoshu: *Jyoshu* historically refers to the area now known as Gunma Prefecture in Japan. Gunma is located to the northwest of Tokyo and is renowned for its beautiful mountainous landscapes, hot springs (*onsens*), and historical sites.

Katakana: *Katakana* is one of the three writing systems used in the Japanese language, alongside *hiragana* and *kanji*. It consists of 46 basic characters, which are based on simplified segments of more complex *kanji* characters. *Katakana* is primarily used for the transcription of foreign words into Japanese, the writing of loan words, onomatopoeia, technical and scientific terms, as well as names of plants, animals, and minerals.

Kiinokuni Hill: *Kiinokuni Hill* is a geographical location in the Akasaka district of Tokyo.

Kikuchi Kan Prize: The *Kikuchi Kan Prize*, named after writer Kan Kikuchi, is a prestigious Japanese literary award recognizing notable contributions to literature and culture, honoring writers for their creative achievements and impact on the literary landscape.

Koban: *Koban* was a type of oval gold coin in Japan under the Tokugawa shogunate, which governed Japan throughout the Edo Era from 1603 to 1868. Initially worth one *ryo* of gold (16g to 18g), the *koban* was considered a symbol of wealth and power.

Kon-Kon: In Japan, the onomatopoeic sound *"kon-kon"* is commonly associated with a fox's bark or cry. This same sound is also used to mimic the sound of a human cough. This overlapping association has given rise to a belief in Japanese folklore: One cough signifies a fox is near, while two coughs denote the fox being far away.

Matsutake Mushrooms: *Matsutake mushrooms*, also known as pine mushrooms, are highly prized and sought-after fungi in Japanese cuisine and culture. These mushrooms grow in symbiosis with the roots of pine trees and are known for their distinctive spicy-aromatic fragrance and earthy flavor. Due to their rarity and unique taste, they are often used in traditional Japanese dishes such as sukiyaki, rice dishes, soups, and hot pots.

Mikan: The Japanese *mikan*, also known as the Satsuma mandarin, is a small citrus fruit with a bright orange, thin, and smooth peel. It is one of the most popular citrus fruits in Japan. *Mikan* trees are often planted on slopes and terraced hillsides facing the sea for optimal drainage, frost protection, and sunlight exposure, all vital for tree health and productivity.

Mino Province: *Mino Province* was located in the central part of Japan's main island, Honshu. Today, this area corresponds to parts of Gifu Prefecture, Aichi Prefecture, and Mie Prefecture. It was known for its scenic beauty, historical significance, and cultural heritage.

Mizusawa Observatory: Founded in 1886, the *Mizusawa Observatory* is situated in the town of Mizusawa, nestled in the Oshu District of Iwate Prefecture in the scenic Tohoku region of northern Japan. Today, it continues to serve as a key center for astronomical research within the National Astronomical Observatory of Japan (NAOJ).

Mogami County, Yamagata Prefecture: *Mogami County*, a former county located in *Yamagata Prefecture* in the northern part of Japan's main island, Honshu. In 2006, it merged with surrounding counties to form Murayama District. It is known for its picturesque landscapes, including mountains, rivers, and agricultural fields.

Moku-Gyo: *Moku-gyo* (wooden fish) is a traditional Japanese percussion instrument used in Buddhist rituals and practices. It is typically carved from a single piece of wood and shaped like a fish with its mouth open. The fish is hollow inside, and when struck with a mallet, it produces a deep, resonant sound that is believed to aid in meditation and mindfulness.

Pagoda: The Japanese *pagoda* is a tiered tower with multiple eaves found in Buddhist temple complexes. Derived from Indian stupas, these structures are traditionally made of wood and serve religious purposes. They typically have an odd number of stories, often five, symbolizing the five elements of Buddhist cosmology: earth, water, fire, wind, and void.

Red and **White:** Japanese fox masks feature *red* and *white*, each with deep cultural significance. *Red* denotes power, protection, and good fortune, with masks featuring red accents embodying the protective and mischievous aspects of fox, warding off evil and bringing prosperity. *White* represents purity, virtue, and protection in Shinto belief, used in festivals to symbolize the benevolent fox spirits serving Inari, the deity of rice, fertility, and prosperity.

Reinun's Meiji Rebel Biography: *Reinun's Meiji Rebel Biography* explores the pivotal roles of Meiji rebels during Japan's transformative Meiji Restoration in 1868. It delves into Japan's modernization and political upheaval, showcasing the rebels' advocacy for change and influence on the nation's future.

Ri: In traditional Japanese measurement, one *ri* is approximately equal to 3.927 kilometers (2.44 miles).

Rice Milling: In Japan, the *rice milling* process typically occurs in early spring following the autumn harvest, preparing the rice for cooking and consumption throughout the year. The freshly harvested rice grains are processed to remove the outer husk or bran, resulting in polished white rice.

Roku-Jizo Statues: *Roku-Jizo Statues*, also referred to as the *Six Jizo Statues*, are a set of six stone Buddhist figures found along roadsides, pathways, or in mountainous regions in Japan. Each statue represents a revered figure in Japanese Buddhism, known for protecting travelers, children, and the deceased.

Sanbaso Puppet: *Sanbaso puppet* is a character in traditional Japanese performing arts, often associated with Noh and Bunraku (puppet theater). This character usually performs a type of ceremonial dance that is meant to bring good fortune or celebrate an auspicious occasion.

Shinano: *Shinano* is a historical province in the region of Nagano, which is located in the central part of Japan's main island, Honshu.

Shoji Screens/Doors: *Shoji screens* are traditional Japanese interior features consisting of wooden frames covered with translucent rice paper. These screens serve as partitions, doors, and windows, allowing natural light to diffuse softly while maintaining privacy.

Soba: *Soba* (buckwheat noodles) is a popular Japanese dish consisting of thin noodles made from buckwheat flour, typically served hot or cold with various toppings.

Tatami Room: A *tatami room* is a traditional Japanese room with flooring made of *tatami mats*, which are woven straw mats known for their softness and durability. Common in Japanese homes and inns, these rooms feature sliding paper doors, low furniture, and a simple, nature-connected design.

Tsukiji Wall: The *Tsukiji Wall* refers to the boundary wall surrounding a residence belonging to the Kishu Domain, a powerful feudal domain during the *Edo Era*.

Waka: Japanese *waka* poetry is a traditional form of Japanese poetry that consists of a specific number of syllables and lines. *Waka* poems are typically composed of alternating lines of 5-7-5-7-7 syllables and explore themes such as nature, emotions, and the seasons.

Wakame Seaweed: *Wakame seaweed* is a type of dark green, edible seaweed with a slightly sweet, delicate flavor and silky texture. Commonly used in Japanese cuisine, it's found in soups, salads, and snacks.

Yotsuya: *Yotsuya* is a district in Tokyo with a rich history and connections to various folklore and ghost stories. It is often portrayed as a mysterious and eerie location in Japanese literature and entertainment.

ABOUT THE TRANSLATORS

Finlay Cameron, a seasoned Japanese-English translator, checker, and proofreader, excels in technical, legal, and audiovisual translation fields. While known for his expertise in technical and legal content, Finlay's foray into literary translation with the enchanting stories of Kenji Miyazawa, Nankichi Niimi, and Kohei Tsuchida showcases his versatility and passion for language. His ongoing project involves a more comprehensive translation of the works of these authors, demonstrating his dedication to bringing their narratives to a wider audience.

John McLean, a British-born Japanese-English translator and interpreter, is recognized as one of Japan's leading interpreters. He also brings extensive experience as a production editor, emcee, film festival talk-show host, and university associate professor in Hiroshima. McLean has worked with world-class athletes like Ai Fukuhara and Kohei Uchimura, renowned actors and models such as Nana Komatsu and Kentaro Sakaguchi, and dignitaries like Kazumi Matsui. Additionally, he has collaborated with media outlets including NBC, CBC, and Al Jazeera. As a seasoned translator and translation educator, exemplified by his work in *Tricksters in the Twilight*, John aims to shape the next generation of Japanese literature enthusiasts and literary translators.

Matatabi Press is on the lookout for fresh talent. If you can answer yes to any of the following questions, don't hesitate to reach out to us at press@matatabi-japan.com:

- Are you a storyteller ready to share your narrative with the world?
- Do you have a passion for developing English graded readers as an EFL/ESL professional?
- Are you a Japanese language expert interested in collaborating on a Japanese graded reader?
- Are you a Japanese-English translator excited about bringing Japanese literature to a new audience?
- Are you a language, literature, education, or translation/interpreting scholar looking to publish your research?

Connect with us to explore exciting opportunities and become a valued member of our team.

Milton Keynes UK
Ingram Content Group UK Ltd.
UKHW020657130824
446895UK00012B/370